BEFORE the JOURNEY
BECAME HOME

BEFORE THE JOURNEY BECAME HOME
COPYRIGHT © 2010 Sowunmi, Zents Kunle
Request for information should be addressed to
Korloki, Inc., P.O. Box 165175, Irving Texas 75016-5175

Cover design by: CreateSpace.com
Interior design: CreateSpace.com
Photographs: K Dukes Photography Dallas, Texas USA

Library of Congress Cataloging-in-Publication Data

Sowunmi, Zents Kunle.

Summary: *The most detailed and remarkable childhood experience ever written by an Immigrant. This writer left nothing on the table, very emotional on the fears, hopes and anxieties of relocation to a foreign land. A non-fiction, humorous, religious, deep in values and historical book of an immigrant who reflects on his early years in Africa and short trip to America, the land that finally became home.*

Copyright © 2010 Sowunmi, Zents Kunle
ISBN-13: 9780615302621
ISBN: 0615302629

Other Books by Zents Kunle Sowunmi

What Happened to Our Democracy?
Humbled by Faith
100 Ways to Laugh
Not a Stranger Anymore
The Fear of Tomorrow
Keep on Going

BEFORE the JOURNEY BECAME HOME

The most detailed and remarkable childhood experience ever written by an Immigrant.

Zents Sowunmi

What Others Are Saying About Zents

"Zents Kunle has been a friend of over 35 years. He is highly determined, intelligent and vast with a good sense of humor. His interest cut across all fields."

Col Olusegun Atanda (Rtd), Lagos, Nigeria

"Kunle is devoted to sharing his knowledge and experiences with humankind. He is a genuine inspiration, as well as, a facilitator for a better world. I am so grateful for our Lagos museum meeting in 1991, and am truly proud to call him a friend."

Tara Crouse, Canada

"Zents, is a man that despite repeated rejections and unfulfilled expectations kept at all times focus and intensity in his goals. His book will enrich your knowledge."

Millie Delgado, US Army

"When I first met Zents I knew he would be different from many of the men I'd met. He had a great sense of humor and was friendly in such a genuine manner. His intelligence and knowledge of numerous subjects kindly overshadowed his friendliness. We could converse on any topic and his love of books and information of any sort shone through. I am proud to call him a friend and honored that he crossed my life's path."

Jacquie Lewis, Dallas, Texas

"Kunle is a friend of several years, a prolific writer and social critics of injustice around the world, especially in Africa. Though far away from his beloved nation, the sufferings of the masses and wickedness of the leaders remain uppermost in his mind."

Biodun Osomo, London, UK

"Kunle is the only guy who can eloquently shed light on four high school students at Lisabi Grammar school, Abeokuta. They are Lobito Brown, Sali "Sample", Innocent and Sopade. They met through destiny and they made the best of the time."

Lobito Brown, South Carolina

Zents Sowunmi

Dedication

I dedicate this book to
the memory of
my late father Michael Olaide Sowunmi
&
My mother Hannah Bolanle Sowunmi
(nee Onifade)

Who jointly sacrificed their lives and comforts
to make sure their children got a good upbringing
through dedication and love to all.

Contents

Foreword

Learning other cultures and people's way of life has always fascinated me. I love meeting people and making new friends. The way each culture does things, such as how we eat, how we dress, how we acknowledge people, the manner in which we worship God, and much more, is not necessarily the "right or better way," it is just cultural differences. It doesn't make one culture right and another culture wrong; it merely shows that we do things "differently."

You will read many intriguing stories such as stories of tortoise, stories of African gods like god of Twins, stories of creating and maintaining great friendships, great family stories, struggles, and almost unbelievable stories in *Before the Journey Became Home*.

In *Before the Journey Became Home*, you'll discover the author's passion and enthusiasm for life, people, his *old* continent (Africa), and his *new* country (America), and his passion for family and friends. You will discover that he has a keen memory, as he remembers many childhood events. Zents

Sowunmi has a good sense of humor. He is a person who remembers family and friends, and has a big heart, and is ready to assist anyone.

Zents Sowunmi is a well-grounded individual with knowledge of many subjects. In *Before the Journey Became Home* you will learn more about politics, friendships, family issues, geography, different religions, business, historical events and all that can enrich your knowledge about Africa, its people, customs, and beliefs.

His whimsical method of imparting knowledge will have you laughing, and occasionally thinking, long after a conversation with him has ended. *Before the Journey Became Home* is a book that will make you laugh out loud, rejoice, and maybe even shed a tear at times. It is a book that will make you feel as though you were right there walking with the author every step of the way on his journey that eventually became home.

Della Faye
Author, Speaker,
Performance Improvement Trainer

Appreciation

Honesty remains unquestionably the foundation of friendship, which is also the lubricant that greases relationship, but when it is exceedingly difficult to tell a friend the truth, the trust is sadly gone. I have protected the identities of some characters in this book because of the positions they are still holding with the government or institutions. The book is never intended to tarnish the image of anyone, but to explain the real me that was often misunderstood as a son, a man, a husband, a brother, and in all a friend.

Ms. Judy Lambert, the Editor of a newspaper in Oklahoma State, was the first editor of this book who used her pen to teach me how to write in the language that people of her community could understand. I am very grateful to her from the deepest corner of my heart, if there is something like that, and to Ms. Erin Russell of Brookhaven College Dallas, Texas, who finished the editing of this book in a very timely manner. I am also indebted to my friends Ginny Cole of New Hampshire who also went through the pages of this book with me, Ms. Jacquelyn Jurkowski, Mrs. Jacquie Lewis, and Mr. Gladstone Adams.

Before the Journey Became Home is a book written by accident that came out of discussions with friends and colleagues, and when the need to write it finally came, it was an expected accident. In this book you will find my undeniable love for my community, and tears and frustrations of a journey that could have collectively been better or should not have taken place at all. But when the need to make a choice of staying or moving on became real, you will understand why I began on the journey that eventually became my home. You will laugh or smile with or at me and sometimes shed tears with me and all the facts mentioned here were never exaggerated, but in all, life to me is fun and full of laughter. If you can see it that way, I believe you will have the value for your time for reading *Before the Journey Became Home*.

Finally, thanks to Della for her commitment to finishing and assembling all that was needed to make the book a reality.

Zents Sowunmi
July 28, 2010

PART ONE

The Trip

Part One
The Trip

*The shortest distance between two points
is equal to a straight line.*

Anonymous

The Trip

Brother, maybe you should relocate to America, Lanre said sarcastically.

"Why?" I asked. His words stung as they sunk into my mind. My junior brother and I were close and he often challenged me to see the reality around me as to the reason he left the country.

In denial of the reality of all the events around me in the last 5 years, I built in layers to consider his proposal. He had been helpful to his big brother over the years which had opened my eyes on the fallen rate of naira to dollar that was going up at an uncontrollable rate in the last years when the military took over government and introduced unscientifically fiscal policy.

I could not imagine the idea of relocation to a foreign land at this "methuselahnic age" of mine, an expression I borrowed from my close friend Bayo. We were both students of Ogun State Polytechnic in the early eighties. The friendship had degenerated over the years due to our inability to manage simple crises that almost broke our families into two. I still dearly, missed some of his antics of communication. Bayo had this traditional wisdom of talking due to the fact that he lived in the heartland of Ibadan City noted for a very deep sense of humor.

I had just celebrated my 40th birthday anniversary on mother Earth in a low profile, with few friends and with a cursory look at the last forty years: it had not been a bed of roses. Hope had been dashed. The presidential election in 1993, which the rich mogul MKO Abiola won was annulled by the military government, had turned sour, and its negative spillover effect had baffled imaginations worldwide.

How could the best and freest election since our independence in 1960 be annulled, was a surprise to every civilized country. Within 10 months, we had three governments under three leaderships; all led to no positive direction. The country was drifting down every day, and the whole business community was abandoned to the mercy of hyper-inflations. Business partners had started hating each other with vengeance, leading to many unwanted court litigations, as most businesses were returning increasing losses; banks were collapsing as the nation continued to witness capital flights from all and sundry.

Hopelessness and lack of direction on where the country was heading pervaded the hearts and minds of the citizens, nothing positive seemed to be moving.

My paint company had gone down. I could see all my working capital disappearing before my very eyes with little or no effort on my part. It was like being on the Titanic ship and watching it sink, but being powerless to shape any positive survival strategies. The whole business community was living in fear, fear of now and of the future, and there was nothing anyone could do.

My company's vehicles were no longer serviceable, without even enough fuel or diesel to run the generator to power our machines for production; workers and employers lived in fear of the present, not even of the future, as the future promised nothing. Since the country was grounded by lack of electricity, most business owners resulted to the use of diesel engines for energy, but diesels were not even available to run the generators. The country's electric company had been paralyzed due to poor management, lack of government funding, and promotion of cronies' employees into management, which deprived the company of effective productivity. This led to a complete breakdown, and in most cases, darkness, throughout the nation.

NEPA, National Electric Power Authority, the name of the only power supply corporation in the country was referred to sarcastically by all, "never expect power always". We had to grease the hands of its officials before we could have electricity supplied for 3 to 4 hours a day. When we have it at all, it was usually half current and probably dull and not adequate to turn on most of our machines that were three phases.

Most industrialists were forced to do the unlikely to get power supply. We greased the palms of the NEPA officials, such was the daily life of an industrialist in Nigeria—Africa's most populous nation and one of the largest world petroleum exporters in the nineties. No bribe, no power supply was the deal; no more, no less.

Zents Industries, a company I started as Zents Enterprises, had started as a one man business until I met Philip a colleague from the Business School at Ibadan; banking and finance was his major. The friendship continued after the program and he had encouraged me to use the government facility of NERFUND, similar to the SBA organization in America, to finance the company.

"You know, given the right connections, you could get up to five million naira in no interest government loans for your company. If you allow me, I can introduce you to one of the directors of NERFUND, who happened to be my client in the bank," Philip said.

Philip was one of the few members of the post graduate class of banking and finance from the University of Ibadan that had climbed up the ladder of success very quickly. He became General Manager of Africa Mortgage Bank a few years after graduation, but he had spent his years with General Mortgage Bank at Lagos, and the experience he brought to the table was good enough to boost his career. It did not take his employer a long time before Philip was made the Managing Director. His office was located in the Victoria Island of Lagos. He became one of the regular faces we saw on television when mortgage issues were raised, we were very proud of his achievement.

"I will be very grateful to you if you can arrange the meeting with this NERFUND man next week," I said.

I left my phone number with him before I went back to Abeokuta a city I had taken as my home since 1979. True to his word, he arranged the meeting, and a week after, I was sitting face-to-face with the man in charge of millions of government money in the Lagos Nigeria division of the organization. Philip was the most powerful man in the banking industry to me.

"I am Joe Chris and I have been briefed," was his way of introducing himself. He extended his hand to shake my hand and I could see his index finger laced with a beautiful ring. He was a man of robust personality at the lower extremities, with a pencil-lined, funny mustache, and a white native Hausa cap to match his smart starched and ironed Dashiki dress. He could not have been more than 40 years of age.

I explained with professional and competent background of a person in the building and chemical industry my business plan and opportunities, strengths and weaknesses available to the new company in a 35 minutes presentation and he was impressed.

He advised me to incorporate Zents Enterprises into a limited liability company from an enterprise, to also appoint more directors into the company, and get back to him. I offered him five percent of the company, as was the practice in those days, which he never rejected nor accepted. He just smiled over the proposal and Philip decided not to be a witness to a situation where good things will be shared without benefiting from it.

"How about me, for introducing you guys?" Philip said, in his deep voice that could pass for those working in the entertainment industry. He used to act in local movies during his days in the University, and on a part time basis, before the pressure of business and banking took him off the stage.

"You could come on board also on five percent ownership," I said.

The NERFUND man excused himself from the meeting, leaving the two of us behind. We planned on how the company, Zents Enterprise, could become a limited liability company. We talked about the registration with government agencies, and the role each one of us was to perform.

I noticed a gleam in Philip's eyes. I never suspected anything. After all, I still have 90 percent of my company, I thought. I was wrong.

"I have an attorney that can incorporate this company for us, and he is a friend of one of the staff here who I would like you two to meet later in the week," Philip said.

"That will be fine, but how well do you think this guy can handle this paperwork, since everything will have to be done at Abuja," I said.

Abuja, the new Federal Capital, had taken the shine and administrative controls from Lagos. All government activities, including company registration and incorporation, seemed to have been transferred out of Lagos.

"Never mind; he has an office in Abuja, and things are now being done by fax these days," he said empathetically. Little did I know I was being conned by the classic scammers.

Benson was the staff member Philip introduced. He was in charge of the Business Development of Africa Mortgage Bank. He was a member of the Celestial Church of Christ, a white garment church, where nobody wears shoes. Members go barefoot during church programs, when in the white garment, whether in and out of church in Lagos. Benson was a well dressed man, trimmed, and a man who appeared to be in charge of his health and figure. He was a man with likeable personality.

Surprisingly, at the next meeting, Philip introduced another staff of his bank as a director, and he was the Chief Accountant of the Bank, an Igbo tribe man. These two new people were reporting to Philip, and he had dominion over their cognitive thinking, but they all appeared to be genuine in thinking and discussion. Again I was wrong.

By the time I saw the Article of Incorporation as registered, I knew I was already in the midst of corporate politics which would reduce my shares or stocks to 50 percent, and divide the rest among the Africa Mortgage Mafia, and it was too late to pull out.

I was now ready to show the members how the politics of business could be better done. I sought advice from those who were veterans in business long before me. It was suggested that the name of Zents be patented by Zents Enterprise as a future antidote against any future board room politics and economic upheaval which the members may try to spring on me.

Believe me; it was not long before the handwriting of intricacies started. That was four years ago. We argued over irrelevances cut unnecessary deal among each other and finally saw the handwriting on the wall that the company might have to be sold, at a time when the inflation was eating up our working capital.

When the Presidential election was finally annulled in 1992 by the then-military President, the spillover effect of it on the economy was enough to destroy most small businesses. Zents Industrial Company was eventually sold. We paid off debts to all our creditors and outstanding workers, and said that it was time for us to move on.

It was a bright and fulfilling morning in August 1996. I had said my prayers and worshiped the Lord in my way with my family; we sang the songs of praises and continued to rejoice in the Lord according to his glory and promises. I had invited a prayer partner all the way from the Eastern part of Nigeria to partake in the night vigil. Her name was Green, and she had remained a good family friend from the time I visited Enugu town few years ago as the Marketing Manager of Niger Cedar Industries.

We were all guests of Royal Hotel in Enugu, and I could recall her enthusiasm in preaching the gospel to me. I had ignored her sermon, but was taken by her beauty and dexterity of her fine motor coordination. Her choice of English language was superb, and I was more interested in her brain and beauty than in her preaching. Ms. Green was a very persuasive preacher, and she was able to communicate the gospel messages to me.

"You need to give your life to Jesus," was all she kept saying as she looked directly into my eyes with a hidden and serious smile of a believer in her eyes. She was one of the many that had influenced my Christian rebirth after my years as a member of the Roman Catholic Church.

Yes, a night vigil, for serious and energy-sapping prayers of faith, for the journey that was only supposed to be for three months or six months at least. That was my reckoning, but it was not to be, the effect of the nose diving economy made me to reconsider my stay in the country.

It was not the practice or custom of my people to announce to the world or the public a journey of such nature. Most things are done with the highest level of secrecy that can be arranged, because of fear of unknown and negative forces, real and unreal, which could lead to a spiritual blockage or cancellation of such a trip.

You cannot blame the society. We have seen many abortive projects and negative events in the past and present. Even the Bible says, when things are working well, pray, and when they are not, you must still pray, and in all things stand by the Lord. This is the secrecy of obedience and close contact with God in a one on one relationship. No middle man, except the man of God, my Priest. These were the standards I abided by. Inside me I feared the Lord, I trembled at the thought of being on the wrong side of his love but I struggled between being right and kindness.

My Yoruba tribe believed in secrecy to the point of annoyance. Some events that would have been discussed openly in the western world were hidden to the level that friendships and trust were offended, but we were all used to it. It was the way of life, and everybody understood this.

On August 4, I set for Lagos from Abeokuta. It would be a two hour trip to the Murtala Mohammed Airport, which was built at the twilight of FESTAC 77, when the country hosted the Black festival of Arts and Culture. One of the last memorable occasions for me at the Airport was when my brother Lanre traveled in 1992, also when Daniel, a close friend of mine, also left the country in 1978 for the United Kingdom.

It would be my first international flight out of the country where I had spent the first forty years of my life. My previous overseas trips had been to other African countries, like Ghana, Sierra Leone, Cameroon, Gabon, Benin, and Togo, and they were by roads. But none of these countries could be compared to the bigger road infrastructures in Nigeria, and it was never in the minds of average Nigerians to consider these African countries as a significant overseas trip.

Lagos Airport was full of travelers, like me, and first time travelers, pretending, like me, so as not to show it to the world. We all wanted to appear normal. Like regular travelers says, "Never show your ignorance or ask stupid questions." We looked at what the next person was doing, just copied it, and everything was okay. That was what I did, until I was in the KLM plane and discovered I was unable to fasten my seat belt.

"Do you think they changed the hook on this seat belt" I asked the person beside me and hiding my ignorance as much as I could.

"They probably did," he said, and he helped.

I was not sure if he knew I was not being truthful, but I could see a faint line of smile on his lips. I was by the window, and could see the beautiful side of Lagos from the buildings and cars on the road. I had the feeling that I would be leaving all behind, I mean everything: family, business, and long time friends and associates. On a journey, posterity will be the judge. I closed my eyes like every other Nigerian or first time traveler, and said the following prayers. Nigerians believe in prayers before anything.

"Oh Lord of Hosts, in Thee I put my trust. Have mercy on me in my journey. Let your love and mercy shine over me and all that I will come in contact with. Let me arrive in good health and be the conqueror, not a victim. Let me be a winner, not a loser, and let your goodwill and protection be all over me and those I will come in contact with. AMEN," I said, in my little way of communicating with God. Sometimes I wish I could be better in prayers but my Catholic background of short prayers did not help either.

I opened my eyes to see the KLM plane take off into the black sky on the first level of the journey to Amsterdam. I looked out through the window but there was nothing to look at. The sky was dark, not even the stars. Nothing, it was all dark. I went into a long sleep. I could not even remember what it would be like to fly over the world's most important Sahara desert in the heart of North of Africa. It was late in the night and there was nothing to see below. I slept.

When the plane landed at the Amsterdam Airport six hours after leaving Lagos, it was a different ball game altogether. The organization was perfect, beautiful, and three times larger than Murtala Mohammed Airport in Lagos. We took a long walk inside the airport. It was very beautiful to see all the shopping stores and booths on both sides, well arranged and bigger in structures than Lagos. I started noticing the differences between Africa and white man's land.

It was not long before we connected with another flight to Minneapolis, United States of America. The plane was different, roomier, and much more comfortable inside than the flight that came from Lagos. I could not remember what happened in the plane, because I spent most of the time sleeping, or wondering if I was doing the right thing leaving everything behind. Nigeria was my first love and just walking away from it was very tough on me.

I was missing my father already, and my children. I remembered the fun of being with my father most nights, sharing, and just talking and keeping his company. But we all knew, since economy was going down, it was not going to last long before my relocation would take place. I was the last to suspect it, but everyone around me knew before I did that I was not meant to stay in the country any longer. My ideas and thinking were mostly strange. I was more of a critic of the system in Nigeria than a follower of corrupt system, and I was losing more of my colleagues to the system than I was gaining. The loss of everything was still fresh and always will be. It hurt like the sharp pain between hemorrhoid and toothache for me to leave everything behind and never to look back or stay connected in the way I would have loved to.

I was influenced by all the reading I had done in the past, and it did not take me long to realize this myself. How strange it could be sometimes, as life could be a mirror, reflecting one's views about everything. Maybe I was right in taking the step to move on. I said maybe. By the time the plane landed at DFW Airport in Dallas, Texas on August 4th 1996, my brother Lanre was waiting for me with a wide smile on his face showing all his premolars. It was our own family reunion even if it meant only the two of us.

PART TWO

The Squirrel in My Yard

Part Two
The Squirrel in My Yard

*Sometimes you pick the moment and some-
times the moment picks you.*

US (D) Senator Richard Durbin 2008

The Squirrel in My Yard

❖ ❖ ❖

"**Y**ou need to do something about this squirrel", Faye yelled at the top of her voice. I had already heard this appeal several times this year since we moved in; she was upset about the constant noise the squirrel was making on the rooftop, which was disturbing her sleep. The squirrel had chewed up the wood, sometimes electric wires and cables, and everything else it could lay its teeth on. The worst of it was this squirrel had developed the habit of peeping through our window as if we were neighbors.

Initially, I had not paid attention to the noise, which seemed faint and sometimes difficult to hear. In my opinion, it should not constitute a problem. But Faye, who worked a graveyard shift, had been trained to listen not only to computer noise, but other noises around her workplace as well. My bedroom was not a workplace. All I wanted was a good night sleep. God knows I find it much easier to sleep than most people. With a 12-hour shift behind me, sleep was not one of my problems.

Faye insisted the scratching noise on the roof made it difficult for her to sleep, claiming this must have something to do with the unwelcome guests. I would have to go up on the roof to know what was going on, meaning I might have to give up my sleep. When Faye wanted something, she would complain and grumble until I got tired and just gave in and did what she wanted.

This is very typical of most women, I thought. Sometimes, I would envy those men who were single. They take all the time in the world to do anything they want without any pressure or outside influence.

One way I enjoyed some relaxation was by taking a short nap on my hammock chair in my yard. It was a habit I learned from my Dad. The "Old Man", as we fondly called him, would read his newspapers and take a short nap in his yard. Perhaps there were times when neighborhood disputes were settled right there in that very yard. As one of the few literates in the community, my father's views were sought at all times.

I used to sit very close to him, listening to most of his opinions and advice to many of the people in our neighborhood. He was an unusual person; a wise man that respected and believed in family values and unity. This concept of his reshaped many homes in our neighborhood, but his generosity was often abused.

Like my Old Man, I did my meditation under the oak tree in the center of my yard. I now understood the joy he found in this type of relaxation. One could read, meditate and be able to conceive new ideas. I could even listen to my heart beating and pounding like a drum against the walls of my ribs, my mind and soul functioning as if I was by the river side. It was heavenly.

I gazed at the sky through the leaves; the rays of light penetrating like sharp arrows from different dimensions. I noticed with rapt attention the changes going on in my yard, from the green grass of the Bahamas trimmed in a circular shape, to the hibiscus plant I brought from Oklahoma during my last vacation.

I never thought it could survive the harsh weather of Texas, though I made a determined effort to water the grass and plant daily. It was very gratifying to watch the plant survive. The oak tree, which I noticed when I bought the property, had blossomed into a graceful shade and acted as an umbrella covering the many events that would take place beneath this tree. I looked at everything within my yard. It was glorious, seeing nature at its best; all was peaceful.

"Oh, my God, no," Faye shouted in a voice that sometimes passed for that of a radio commentator. She does, in fact, have radio announcer credentials; a career she never pursued.

She almost ran into the squirrel in her new Toyota Tundra. She loved the truck because of the shiny black color. With its protruding nose, the Tundra seemed to stretch miles ahead on the road.

"It gives me imposing confidence against all other vehicles on the road," was her comment a few weeks after she purchased Toyota's "new thing" for Texas roads; a state we often refer to as "Everything is big in Texas."

She was scared at the thought of killing this ever-intruding and unwelcome pest. She had started reading books on squirrels, which was usually her habit when faced with any issue.

As for me, I had gotten used to seeing the squirrel move around my yard, eating the grass and nuts voraciously, and moving gracefully on my window sill as well as in the garage without any fear of me or my presence. I had come to accept this squirrel as a member of the family. Fear was not part of this squirrel's character. It would move around effortlessly, sometimes coming very close to my legs as if we were friends.

It somehow amazes me, because squirrels in Africa where I was born, and which I had spent the first forty years of my adult life, cannot be close to humans, probably due to the fear that they may be killed, which is true. They will. I knew what we called them in Africa, "Bush Meat," which was very common in most of the ports or restaurants in the motherland. In most areas, they are considered special delicacies, particularly in Abeokuta, from Mama Kola to Eji Alamala, which were often requested for back home in most local restaurants. But this is America, and the thought of these spicy and juicy bush meats moving around without fearing molestation amazed me.

"No one can kill any of those squirrels here," Lanre said.

"Really," I had said in surprise.

Lanre had been in America before me and I was able to get firsthand information on American interest in animals or pets.

In America freedom is even extended to animals. I wonder why this is not the situation in the motherland. I often wonder if the performance of the squirrel could be likened to the folklore we grew up with in Africa about the intelligence of the tortoise, on which so many stories have been compared, ranging from his bald head, to his disfigured shell. It was very interesting to listen to those teachers in those days.

Mr. Tony, our favorite folk storytelling teacher by all accounts, would clear his throat before starting any tortoise stories. All of us would be eager to listen. With rapt attention, we waited for him to start and in most cases, we students, never wanted the stories to end.

"There was a famine in those days," he said. "There was no water, nothing from the farm to sustain the human race, and food was only available in heaven." Tortoise said, "But I have no feathers to fly." He set up a meeting of all the birds, and asked them to donate one feather each, so that he could take them to the source of food.

Over three hundred different types of birds attended the meeting, and each donated a feather. Tortoise was cunning. He wanted it all, so invented a story that in heaven a first time visitor must be given a new name and a new identity. Their earthly names and identity would not be acceptable in heaven. Each bird believed Tortoise's story and each was given a new name. Tortoise, for himself, chose the name "all of you," and was quite proud of his choice.

On the day of the flight to heaven, all the birds' family members gathered to wish their loved ones a safe trip, and hoped they would return with enough for everyone on earth to eat.

Tortoise, in his new feathered regalia, looked like the king of the birds. It was a very joyful gathering as the birds and Tortoise began the trip, like the astronauts, to ascend to heaven.

Finally, they got to heaven and there was plenty of food. They were well received. The heavenly people believed in their minds that Tortoise, with his Biblical, Joseph-like appearance, must be the king of all the visitors. Most importantly, they believed this because he was addressed as "all of you", and treated differently, with respect.

When the food was served at the dinner table, Tortoise asked in his mischievous manner, "Who can have all of these foods?"

The food server replied, "All of you."

Tortoise looked at his colleagues in his greedy manner and told them, "You must wait for your turn."

All the birds waited and waited. No other food came. Also, when drinks came, Tortoise repeated the same question. "All of you," he was told. He was the only one that drank and ate. The other birds only had his leftovers.

All the birds were so unhappy that they demanded the feathers they had given him be returned and flew back home, leaving the featherless tortoise behind. But he told one of the birds to tell his wife to place all their soft mattresses and clothes on the ground outside, so that he could jump and have a safe landing. The birds, on arriving home, told Tortoise's wife her husband had acquired a magical power, and she should spread all the hard objects outside for a special and historical landing.

Tortoise, up in heaven looking down on earth, saw the objects his wife was spreading and thought they were as he had requested, so he jumped, and landed on his back, and had his shell broken to pieces. He did not die, but to this day he never had a smooth shell."

As if Mr. Tony would not have a solution to all questions, one of us had asked how the Tortoise's shell was repaired.

"Tortoise was taken to the only surgeon in the community, and his shell was repaired with the scum which smelled like human feces. Tortoise would not take the smell, which made the scum to do a shady job on his back; hence Tortoise never had a smooth back." Mr. Tony explained

Such were the funny stories we listened to as kindergarten and primary school students in those days.

I have occasionally imagined how palatable this little squirrel creature would look on Foofoo (a type of mashed potato or yam) with vegetable soup, with me crunching and swallowing down this highly tasteful, nutritious protein, and washing it down my throat with a bottle of Guinness beer. The above idea of mine may be opposed to the law on animal Bill of Rights, which may prohibit killing these little creatures. As far as I was concerned certain laws here protect animals.

I've often looked this cute little squirrel eye to eye from a very short distance, both of us appearing to enjoy this eye to eye gazing friendship. The squirrel has a beautiful and hairy long tail, which it often wags in admiration, enjoying the beauty of its environment, or while sitting around eating nuts, its favorite pastime. It stands on its two hind legs, playing with its forearms, occasionally looking left and right as if unsure of its environment. It moves gracefully, and has the potential to be very fast, and smooth. Watching as it climbs tall trees effortlessly, to me, was the most interesting aspect of this little creature.

After each climb, I could hear the squirrel make a sound, as if congratulating itself, and see it wagging its tail in support of this view. In the midst of its friends, the squirrel stands taller, majestically, and elegantly built, with a peacock like tail. I wonder what it might be like to touch the tail.

I noticed this squirrel had many friends. My yard, on some occasions, would play host to one or two other rabbits and woodpeckers from nearby. They moved around as if I had given them permission. Sometimes I wonder just how sociable the squirrels were. I would watch them jump playfully, run around, and chase one another. They seemed not to have a care in the world.

This assumed peace was often disturbed when my neighbor's cat would show up. Who wanted to befriend the cat, especially when the cat was black and ferocious looking? Each time the cat would appear, the squirrel would quickly climb the tree. Birds would fly away in every direction, and the rabbits would speed off, leaving the cat wondering why it was not trusted.

Being from the motherland, I consider squirrel to be edible for human consumption. I had limited knowledge on policies of animal control in the United States. America apportions rights to everyone, including animals. This is rather unheard of in most third-world countries. From what I could understand, there is a bill of rights for animals which varies from state to state. Texas is very strict and protective of animals; you might need a license for fishing and hunting in Texas.

In most third-world countries, different types of animals are eaten. In China, I heard it is even a delicacy to eat lizards, which would be taboo to the Yoruba. Indeed, it is unacceptable to over two-hundred tribes in this great country south of Sahara to eat lizards.

On this particular day, Faye raised her voice a bit higher than usual.

"We will only have lunch after we have taken care of this squirrel issue."

I got the message.

I bought one big cage and five smaller ones from Home Depot, with the hope of catching this squirrel alive. I took the advice the animal control department at Home Depot could offer.

I hooked the trap to the flower pot, and placed nuts at the far end of the trap to act as bait for the squirrel. I was excited with the idea of trapping this little rascal, which would put a stop to all the damage it had caused. Of course, however, I hoped to impress Faye with my expertise on how animals are trapped back home in Africa. I was wrong.

My little friend turned out to be smarter than I anticipated. It probably sensed danger in finding nuts in a place out of the ordinary. It jumped over each of the traps, as if the nuts I had carefully placed there didn't even exist. After each jump, the squirrel would turn around, gaze at me, and seemingly mock me for thinking it was stupid enough to fall into such a trap. I felt as if I had betrayed the trust it had in me. But, as a home owner, I did not intend to turn my property into "Neverland", allowing little animals to take over like Michael Jackson had at his estate in California.

Up to that point, the squirrel had eaten up part of the wood on my house, allowing it to live comfortably along with other creatures in my attic. This did not go down well with me. It was like sharing an apartment without collecting rent. It was not acceptable to me.

I bought lots of mothballs and placed them in the attic, hoping that would make it uncomfortable. The smell was horrible and the moth balls were poisonous. It worked for about two weeks, and then the squirrel was back again. This time, I assumed, with an understanding of its boundaries. It was no longer comfortable with me, probably having received a message from some squirrel relatives of his, warning him of the need to be very careful around this black man from Africa.

After that, I would no longer stand gazing aimlessly at the rodent, but would chase it around until it climbed a tree. It was more of an exercise for me now. I littered the ground with mothballs, which made it difficult for the squirrel to move around at all, so it stayed on the trees. It probably felt sad and restricted, and a little uncomfortable around me.

I noticed that it no longer wagged its tail at me, which I had admired so much, probably due to the strained relationship. Its friends, the rabbits and woodpeckers, probably sensing the danger, never showed up again. However, the black cat never stopped coming around.

I missed being entertained by the rascal, but I managed to keep the value of my property. And when the house was sold, the squirrel was an added value to the new owner. I often drove along the road years later just to see if the squirrel was still there. Once I got a glimpse of a squirrel on the tree but could not be sure if it was indeed the same. It would be funny to ask. This squirrel was jumping and eating nuts like the one I had known.

PART THREE

Old Man

Part Three
Old Man

*Papa, if only you knew how much
I love you, maybe you
would have stayed a little longer than you did.*

*-Zents Sowunmi
November 19, 2007*

Old Man

My father Michael Olaide Sowunmi, fondly called Michaeli by his childhood friends, of whom he had many, was an ex-soldier. He loved the job and never stopped telling us, what it was like in the Army during the colonial days, particularly in the Gold Coast, now known as Ghana, one of the sixteen countries in West Africa.

The soldiers in the colonial services wore knickers, not long pants like they do today. There was a photograph of him in his Army uniform displayed in our living room. He was handsome and a ladies' man in his days. He was six feet tall, an athlete and a great soccer player of his days, but the military was his passion and first love. I sometimes wondered if I should have joined the military like he did.

The military of the past, unlike now, was a career for those who had no family to give them a head start in life, and my dad never really knew his father. Along with my mom, they used to thrill us with the stories about their experiences in all the military locations they ever worked. He served in an administrative capacity in the British Frontier, in locations such as the Gold Coast, and in areas like Zaria and Maiduguri in the northern part of Nigeria, and Ibadan and Ogbomosho in Southern Nigeria. Nigeria was a name given to the people around the River Niger by the wife of Lord Luggard the British Governor General, the colonial Administrator in 1914. It was the left over land used as a slave market before the Berlin Conference of 1885 in Germany.

I was born in the Ekotedo area at Ibadan, one of the early settlers' spots for those whose families and ethnic roots had family root connections with Abeokuta. It was very common to find most of the settlers addressing each other as family members, as it was the practice in those days, but in reality they were not related.

Ibadan City in the west part of Nigeria grew with amazing rapidity in the 18th Century. It was the city for all the soldiers of old Oyo Empire before the advent of British authority in Nigeria. It was a city with a deep sense of humor, which is what it takes to fit into the society. It was part of the culture of the people to be humorous, at least to the outsiders; a city with a different way of pronouncing the English and Yoruba languages. 'Chickens' is pronounced as sickens, 'shooting stars' as suiting stars; the name of their favorable football team in African soccer in the seventies. Their choice of words and pronunciations was very unique among the whole Yoruba tribe.

My early years in this city rubbed on me and my ways of life. Most of my speaking sounds humorous to most people; unknowingly I was only a product of the city where I grew up. I could not see anything wrong in it or the people of Ibadan.

I was almost 35 years old when I went with my father to our village, Eriki Odofin, in the heart of Oba County in Ogun State, Nigeria. The whole population was not more than 500 people, though there were smaller villages within a few miles radius. Eriki Odofin, with its spiritual headquarters in Abeokuta, the hometown of all Egba ethnic of the Yoruba, was an important and historically small but powerful area in the Egba community.

I had heard the name of the village almost from the time I could speak, or understand how community was defined among the people of the Yoruba tribe. I grew anxious and full of expectations when father announced he was taking me, his first son, to this very historical village.

I told my children and wife about the journey to the village of my origin, and the birthplace of my ancestors. The trip in my car, if we had a good road, would be a 40 minute drive, God willing; instead it took more than two hours due to the condition of the road which was full of potholes, sometimes filled with mud and water, due to the lack of a drainage system on most Nigerian roads. The road was lined with beautiful mahogany trees and thick forests.

There were no streetlights from the satellite villages nearest to the road, but we could feel the human life around us in spite of the darkness. Most of the houses were built with reddish mud, sometimes, reinforced with bamboo trees to strengthen the structures of the buildings. The uncemented walls were laced with windows that were very small. Each building could not be more than the fifteen hundred square foot. Most of the roofs lacked the modern sheet, and the visible use of palm fronts on all buildings was carefully weaved to direct water from leaking into the rooms. In most cases it was different from what we have in the cities.

It was uncommon to see a house near the road. One would have to exit off the road and travel two hundred yards or more before reaching a village or home.

The fear during the time of slave trade had prevailed over most of the villages set up in Africa. The scene could pass for a nice location for hunting of wild game. Acceptable animals like antelopes and gorillas, but definitely not lions or other carnivorous wild animals, could be seen crossing the road once in a while, which is the reason most of the people were either farmers or hunters.

My father did not talk, or mention any story to me about the village until we got there. He did that, probably, to prepare my mind, and to allow me to have a spiritual and natural feeling for the community. It was his nature to allow me to assimilate the environment.

I could see the villagers; some were farmers and traders, walking along the road carrying on their heads some of their farm products, like cassava, yam and maize, which they spread out on both sides of the road.

The villagers who had a little bit of money or had a contact in the bigger cities, like Lagos or Ibadan, used bicycles to move around. They were often envied by their peers who were working to attain the same status. It was a form of status elevation to own a bike among your peers in the village. It was even rumored that most villagers with bikes often take a second wife as a status symbol.

"Welcome to Eriki Odofin," was a sign posted about 600 meters into the village. About 500 meters from the village entrance was the elementary school that served about ten neighboring villages. The school built with mud had seen years. It was not painted or cemented like every other building.

The rough road to the village led directly to the house of the village chief, who is often referred to as "Baale." He holds the administrative control of the village and reports to the Abeokuta central community under the Alake of Abeokuta, the paramount ruler of Egba Land.

It was the custom for no one to enter the village without first paying homage to the village Chief "Baale." We followed the tradition bringing our gifts to the village Head. We parted with soulful positive works on how my late Grandfather supported the community, in unity with other villages around, during the "kiriji wars." The positive role of grandfather in his community made me curious to learn more about his life.

Far down the road, directly paralleled and to the right of my late grandfather's dilapidated compound, was the graveyard where my grandfather was buried. It was a very simple and humble grave, simply marked, "Sowunmi Baba Mokoloki."

Mokoloki, a small riverside village, was the place of his trade. He was also a fisherman and boat captain who spent almost his entire life between Eriki Odofin his village, and Mokoloki, a village almost five miles away; taking passengers and gaining new customers during his travels.

Grandfather had left in search of greener pastures from his village Eriki to Mokoloki, which was the tradition in his days. This tradition began sinking into my mind and heart on this first visit. Little did I know at that time, how God would lead me to also seek greener pastures twelve thousand miles away from home; in his own case which was just five miles.

A journey of five miles was like a day's trip since most of it was done on foot. He had established a good reputation for himself, both in the village and among his customers who were using Ogun River, the only navigable river for any journey to Lagos. His job was to take them across the river and back in the evening.

Mokoloki community loved his attitude and talents, and good customer service which were laced with affections and feelings of his clients and clientele. They decided to compensate him with five acres of land on which he built the family house for his only wife, my grandmother.

As a result of his relocation to Mokoloki, he never had to go back to Eriki Odofin after a day's work. Strange things happened to his growing family. He lost 12 of his 13 children. Western medicine was not available during that era and deaths were either attributed to witchcraft or bad luck. Nobody realized the importance or role of Christian faith or modern medicine as regards infant mortality.

Much like the history of western medicine associated with witchcraft in England in the 17th century, it was the same in Africa. Nobody could actually determine what led to the death of these 12 children. All we knew was that they all died, not in one day, but one after the other. Nobody kept any statistics of how and when they died, they just died. That was all we, the living children of my dad, were told. If she never had the training for simple health care precaution we will never know.

It was the practice in Africa to bury the dead very close to the house. Cemeteries came with western education or Christianity. What may have looked like a cemetery could have been what was called an "evil forest," which was a dumping ground for people who died from leprosy or mysterious circumstances. There was nothing in place in Africa during that time to compare to a cemetery of today.

Some people were even buried in the center of their living room, with the belief that the spirit of the dead would guide the house and be a center to settle disputes among family members. In most families with spiritual connections to Masquerades, the spirits of the dead could be evoked and it was celebrated with candor and honor.

Masquerades, or locally called Egungun was an important aspect of the lives of the Yoruba before the advent of Christianity. The costume or outfit could be compared to the dressing of Santa Klaus or Halloweens in the western world. Some families believed the spirit of the late ancestors would always guide the home and protect them from any spiritual attack. A designated member of the family put up the Egungun costume and talked in a deeper rolling voice to express the expectation and decision of the dead to the people.

There was no court of law except the three highest levels of court in the land. The family head, the village head in council, with his chief, and the courts of God through our traditions. According to the belief of the society Shango, god of thunder, is still the most feared of all the gods in Africa; particularly among the Yoruba.

It was a belief among the Yoruba that any man can swear falsely any oath using the Bible or Koran and get away with it, but never with the emblem of Shango the Supreme god of justice. There was the story of a man accused of stealing who was to exonerate himself by swearing with the emblem of Shango to determine his innocence. He falsely told a lie while holding the emblem, and was reportedly struck down with thunder and lightning. We do not mess with Shango or discuss it. Most of the worshipers of this god dressed in red costumes; unless you belong to this group, red attire is not a favorite dress among the Yoruba.

Shango, which the Igbo tribe in the Eastern part of Nigeria also called Amadiora, was a powerful tool for court administration of justice in Africa. Despite the Christianity in the west and east parts of Nigeria, we still do not mess with Shango. Up till today, nobody is willing to test this local god which was exported to most of the Latin American countries, particularly Cuba and Puerto Rico during the slave trade in the

18th century. The most appropriate thing would be to stay away from the believers of this religion, which was the choice of my father and his uncle. We were all Christians and my father, through the faith of his mother, was a staunch Catholic. Then we, the children became Roman Catholics.

My dad showed me the 150 acres of land; his only inheritance.

"My father left this land and building for me. Make sure we do not lose it," he said.

The building on the land was already dilapidated and the whole community looked tired. I cannot remember if the buildings in the whole community were even painted. The site was horrific taken into consideration that I was used to life in the city. There was no electricity, no single paved road. The buildings were all falling apart. They were built with red mud and roofed with old, rusted roofing sheets and some with palm fronts. But this is my source, my link and origin as a black man from Africa.

I looked around the village with discomfort, at the condition of my people, who may never know what is happening beyond the shores of the river Ogun that passed behind them. I could now see why my father's uncle took him away with his mom to live with him at Ibadan and later at Ile Ife, a city known for agricultural produce in the 1930's. My grandmother had already lost 12 children.

Her baby brother, Chief Shoyoye, sensed the same tragedy might happen to her only surviving child, my dad. Chief Shoyoye, my great Uncle legally relocated my grandmother, who was blind or optically challenged, and her only son to Ibadan City. My father attended St. Patrick Primary School, where he was much older than the other students. A few years later they relocated to Ile Ife, the cradle of the Yoruba race in Africa.

My dad's education came from his uncle, from the time he arrived at Ile Ife to the time he went to Ilesha Grammar School, a few miles away from Ife. By the time he was in the school, father was already close to 18 years in age. This may not be exact; as he did not know the year he was born, we had to guess or speculate his age.

His uncle, Chief Shoyoye, had started life as a salesman in Lagos and was one of the first to accept western education in Nigeria. He was known to sell neckties to the upper class people in Nigeria, and at one time in his life he was a commission agent and tailor for the Nigeria police force.

He was one of the best dressed men who ever lived during his time and a practical business man. He loved women, and by the time he died at age of 87, he had gone through 12 women and 17 children. He had no patience for lazy people. Hardworking and very resourceful, he had a temper. It was often advised to stay a little bit away from his reach, particularly if what one was saying did not align with his ideas. Years later I saw a firsthand encounter of the result of his temper and damages done.

My father had taken me to see him when he came to Ibadan on a visit. It was the custom to prostrate on the floor when greeting your elders. As years of polished education were creeping into fabric of the Yoruba custom, prostration was gradually reduced to just bowing and bending when we greeted our elders. My uncle was old fashion and I was not told of his conservative behavior. I did what was known to me as normal; I bowed a bit and bend to show respect.

"Come closer to me" Uncle Shoyoye said.

I did not expect what happened next. In the presence of my father he slapped me, he used uncomplimentary words on my father for not given me proper home training.

I could not take it anymore. The stubborn Idowu and rascality in me came out immediately,

"If you dare touch me again you will see," I said with my eyes all red as I walked out of his living room.

"Laide, where did you get this little rascal?" Uncle Shoyoye challenged my father.

His words were laws to my family and no one had ever challenged him before. Laide was a short word for Olaide, which was the way his uncle called him. He was surprised at this new development.

"He is just an ignorant little child," Father said. He appealed to his uncle to temper mercy on the young boy.

"He must have taken after his mother," My father added.

Mothers in Africa, or among the Yoruba, always take the blame when fathers or an elder disagrees with the behavior of any adolescent. This matter was not even mentioned at home because my maternal grandmother was with us then. I never saw my uncle again nor visited him in Lagos.

Dad, Education, School and Early Years

My Dad remembered the good time he had as a student of Ilesha Grammar School. He made good and lifelong friendships with the Farotimi and a host of others, until, for some reasons, his uncle Chief Shoyoye stopped his education in high school class four. It was a powerful setback and bitter experience, which changed the relationship and affection he had for his uncle. His best friend at school was Julius. Together they started an import and export company named after themselves as Julio-Micho Enterprises.

It took years of pain and sadness for him to get over his arrested education, and with his aged and blind mother to care for he was forced to move to the employment market. He became a teacher in a primary school and relocated to Ibadan. He was there for almost four years, learning how to be a stenographer and bookkeeper, until he visited Lagos where he met my mother.

Presumably at the age of 25, and as the only surviving son of his mother and late father, marriage was the only option to continue the family lineage into the future. He was under constant pressure from his mother to marry and have children at least to save the name of the family from extinction.

I had asked him one day while he was in a good mood to tell us how he met my mother. It was a funny incident, comparable to my mother's behavior today. My mother was a no-nonsense lady in her days. No man was ready to approach her, because her mouth was smart. Other women her age were already married, and when my dad saw her, he was warned of the likely effect of his proposal if he dare approach her.

"Do you have job to support a wife?" Mother said.

Dad had prepared himself for the worst before he approached her.

"Yes. I have a job and I am a very responsible teacher from Ibadan City" he said with confidence.

The City of Ibadan was the center of Yoruba politics and the citadel of western education with the first University in Nigeria since 1948, and those from there were expected to be knowledgeable and smart. Teachers were well respected in those days. They served as foundation and custodians of our values and oneness of family in our society, and that probably paved the way for him to win respect from his wife to be. They dated for a year before the marriage took place in Lagos.

He moved his young wife to Ibadan from Lagos and within a year of marriage they were blessed with my beautiful sister, Abosede, a full-of-life little kid. She was the joy of the family. My father became a changed person. The responsibilities of parenthood were increasing, along with the stress of the responsibilities at home with his mother's declining health. He could not support everyone with the little salary he received as a primary teacher so he did what most people of his time did, joined the military then called the British/West African frontiers. He was posted to Buuku in Maiduguri in the Northeastern part of Nigeria very close to Chad Republic. He began a career that made him a stenographer within the Army, and was relocated a few years later to Gold Coast now called Ghana in West Africa.

Five years was a long time in the Army in those days, and it was all the years he spent with the British and West African frontiers. Eventually my father retired from the military at a relative young age, and still with enough energy, returned to his uncle and together they managed the cocoa produce, at Ile Ife. The sudden change of career from Army to civil life was greatly influenced by the health of his mother who died a few years later.

His Life as a Civil Servant

Years later Papa joined the civil services and worked in the agriculture department, in the registry or administrative capacity; a career that took him to Agege, Lagos, Ibadan, Ado Ekiti, Ilaro, Owode and Abeokuta. He also worked in the tax office until he retired to his hometown. His job had taken him, in addition to the above cities, to most major cities all over the country and some West African countries.

Sometimes, I would sit at my dad's feet and listen to his epistle of when he was a member of the British/West African Frontier in the Old Gold Coast, and his life with his uncles when the Cocoa business was everything to them at Ife.

He was a much respected person in our community in Abeokuta, in Ogun State of Nigeria. I never knew how great this love and respect was until he had a stroke and was admitted to the hospital. He was visited by all and sundry. He was like a father to all. I recollect a scene in which a popular and fearsome native doctor, living within two blocks from my family's home, visited my dad on his sick bed.

"I can see witches surrounding him. They are ready to share his human anatomy among themselves unless you all perform some form of ritual," he said.

"What do we do now?" asked "Mama Idowu" as my mom was fondly called. It is against African or Yoruba culture to address a parent of anybody by name. You are called by the name of the children's mama or baba of the child; in my case she was fondly referred to as Mama Idowu.

"Well we will need over five-thousand naira to buy goats and other things for sacrifices, and the money must be collected tonight," said the native doctor, looking around and gnashing his teeth, as if the ritual must be done immediately with the approval of the anxious and ferocious witches in attendance.

"In this case I will have to ask you to wait until my son Idowu gets back. It is only 9 o'clock in the night now," Mother said.

She looked at the door, wondering if Idowu would show up right away. They all waited patiently for me. I showed up at the Catholic hospital Lantoro, the only modern hospital in Abeokuta despite years of exposure to western education. Coming from the nearby town of Sango Otta a commercial center for business, in the state of Ogun, I was told of my dad's condition immediately as I entered the city.

Fear gripped me. I could not stand the thought of losing my father. It was like the whole world was crumbling beneath my feet. I began to sweat profusely, thinking of all the good things my father did for me. We had come a long way from difficulties and despair to something, from emptiness to fullness, and from no family to a family of almost twenty, with grandchildren and cousins. At this moment I realized that father, "Baami," as I have always called him, must not die now.

I entered the Lantoro hospital room to see my helpless father on the bed. He could not even speak clearly. His eyes were rolled back and he was barely alert. The right upper extremity of his body was paralyzed. For the first time, I realized how close my father was to death. The man I grew up knowing as strong, energetic, and always on the move, now lay helpless and near death upon the hospital bed.

I was shaken with the fear of becoming a fatherless son. Dad was a man of strong character, heavily set with a shining mustache that I used to admire. I could not imagine him without his mustache, which is probably why I keep the same type of mustache today.

I came out to meet this native doctor after listening to his epistle on the witches. I asked the question bothering my mind.

"Can you ask the witches to hold on till tomorrow since all banks are closed right now?" The country did not operate ATM or banking system in those days.

"No, we have to have the money now or he will die," he declared.

I suspected foul play. Of course, I was suspicious of this man. I returned to my father's bedside. In faith, I laid my hand on his head as a Christian according to **James 5:14-15** and prayed to God to challenge the belief of the native doctor.

I came out of the hospital room after the prayer and looked directly into the eyes of the witch doctor.

"If the old man survives, it will be a shame to you and your god."

He was not prepared for this boldness and his authority as witch doctor has never been challenged in our community. He scratched the tip of his tongue with the red feather believed to be quoted with powerful voodoo and made a defensive remark.

"By the powers of the mothers of the witches he cannot survive" he said.

I looked him directly in the eye for a few seconds, and my faith was rekindled without fear of his power or anyone around.

"It does not matter, he would not have died as a young man anyway" I said. Father was 67 years then.

"Let us see" he said, as he walked away with his entire reddish bag on his left hand and murmuring some incantations.

I was not ready to give money to any devil. Papa survived, and the native doctor moved out of our neighborhood in shame.

The community, out of generosity, made it easy for us, my father's children, to pay his hospital bill. Everyone with money tried to outdo the other, and those without money showered us with affection.

My father had ten children by my mother. I was the fourth in the line. The name "Idowu" was given to me due to the manner in which I was born. A male child born after a set of twins is given this name as tradition within the Yoruba tribe demands.

It is against our tradition to let the world know the number of children in your family. It is the belief that witches may not be happy with you, and may cause you to lose the children. However, my family refused to believe this. My father had other children, but only one was known to us.

Anike, his second daughter from his second wife, was his favorite after my sister. We all knew this due to the nature and manner in which she was born. A doctor had told my father that my mother may not be able to bear children again after the way her two set of twins had died. My father, raised as an only child himself, was not satisfied with having my sister as his only child. He remembered being unable to know his other brothers and sister, whom had all died when he was young. He decided to take a second wife who gave birth to his daughter, my half-sister Anike, meaning "the one to cherish." He was still in search of a son to bear the name of father.

In the 1950's in most African countries, witchcraft was rampant, or at least the belief was common. The story of Orofo the bird was quite popular. Orofo had two children and was busy announcing to the whole world that his house was full of kids. Because of this, the children were consumed by witches.

This superstition caused the Yoruba people to never count or give the number of their children in public again. If you asked a Yoruba today, he would say, "Let us just thank God for his blessings." But he will never reveal the number of his children in public.

After 35 years in government service, my father retired from his job as a career civil servant. We were moved to the new state Abeokuta which became the State capital. In his entire lifetime, he was one of those who believed loyalty and honesty were virtues, a thing he passed to his children.

My dad contributed to the establishment of a new government activity set up in many villages and towns, until he finally retired in 1983. He belonged to the old generation of loyal and faithful government officials, being sincere in everything.

Father kept a good diary of everything, including every experience and event that happened to him, both good and bad. In his records, he entered every penny we sent him monthly, and sometimes weekly. In all, he was the man each one of us, his children and neighbors, could trust with our money, values, and secrets. In all, Papa was a father to everyone in our community.

PART FOUR

My Mama

Part Four
My Mama

Mother's love is the fuel that enables a normal human being to do the impossible.

Marion C. Garretty

My Mama

How old are you mama? I asked. At a time I was considered relatively too young to ask such audacious questions.

"I don't know," she said smiling.

At the time of my mother's birth, there was neither a legal record nor any educated person in her village appointed to record the years of birth. Life's events were used as a point of reference to guess the likelihood of age of which most events were based on oral history.

Due to this, it was difficult to establish a clear date of birth for most people of her generation. However, from our calculations, she could have been born in 1924. On each side of her cheek is the traditional Egba tribal marks beautifully done to reflect her position as the first born of the family, that was the custom of our people, a system that has now been eroded with western education. The most beautiful set of teeth one could imagine, like a stallion my mother was taller and imposing than most of her peers.

She was a very strong woman, very loving. All of us called her "Maami," which is more like the literary meaning for mommy or mother. To her children, 'Maami' was more modern than "Iya mi," a slogan I found to be the same among the Hispanics when I relocated to New York years later. As time went on, her place of work became her appellation, and so she was addressed as Mama Ake. Ake was the place she later had her store, when the whole family finally relocated to the City of Abeokuta in 1986.

In all, she was a woman of strong personality, stern in words and action, and if she loved you, she would give you her "eyes." Many of the extended family members took advantage of her in terms of money and property. All she wanted was a simple, basic life. The rest she chose to give to those who needed it most, believing that God would provide whenever there was a need.

We ended up with cousins and nephews in all the areas we lived. Many became richer but poor in love. My mother, however, was all I had when things were not working well for me. I could tell her my inner thoughts and feelings more than I could with my father. My name Idowu was associated with the way my mother was addressed more than any of my brothers or sisters at the early stages of our youth.

Mother was the firstborn of Chief Imam Onifade, a Muslim leader in her village Alagbon, very close to Wasimi on Lagos Abeokuta road. She grew up to read and memorize the verses of the Koran like all Muslims. The focus was to go to Mecca and fulfill the entire requirement, as demanded by the Islamic faith.

My maternal grandmother, Loosade in full meaning Olorisade, (or the one who served the traditional gods is here) was neither a Christian nor a Muslim. My maternal grandfather never tried to convert his wife Loosade to Islamic faith, because it was the condition before he was allowed to marry her. She worshipped the gods of Twins. Loosade never said much in her life and no one dare to cross her way either. She was a tool for her gods and that was what she remained until she passed on.

We, the Yoruba, believe that worship of twins was appropriate at the time of my grandmother. According to Wikipedia, the Yoruba have the largest concentration of twin births in the world: 45 to every 1000 births as against 33 to every 1000 births in the United States of America. In the period of my grandmother, twins were regarded as gods. In some parts of Nigeria they were regarded as strange births among the people of Calabar or Efiks. Twins were often killed until Mary Slessor, a Christian from Europe, came to preach and changed the belief systems of the Efiks.

Later in life, I realized why I was my grandmother's favorite. I was born as Idowu, the male child after the twins. All children named Idowu are considered to be troublemakers, aggressive and spiritually inclined, by the Yoruba belief. All *Idowu's* were supposed to have "Ikere", or an unusual ear, according to the custom, a thing I noticed with my left ear. How it got there remained inscrutability to me and my Christian parents. By custom, people tend to address me as "Idowu Ogbo Abikire leti," which means 'Idowu with an unusual ear" and if an Idowu did not have an unusual ear at birth, the community would have one ear ring implanted on one side.

The Yorubas consider twins to be special children from God. This meant, Twins are believed to have spiritual powers which can create luck and financial prosperity or otherwise. They are more treated specially than those of single birth. Due to this belief, no one wanted to mess with the wishes of the twins, or that of Idowu, the male child after the twins, because of the likelihood of negative repercussion.

They were considered more like gods. In some very primitive environments, as the one my grandmother grew up in, they were worshipped, making my grandmother, and other mothers of twins, disciples of the gods of twins. Until Christianity and Islamic conviction were planted among the Yoruba tribe, it was acceptable. Nothing was wrong with being a disciple of the god of twins, or any other gods.

We loved to go to the village to stay with my maternal grandparents during school vacation, along with my sister, Bose, who had lived with my grandmother when she was very young. Maami, along with the twins and my sister Bose, had stayed in the village her first five years. Mother and dad had separated, and mother had gone back to her village, they lived together until dad returned for his wife.

It was a sad event in the life of my father and my mother, the twins died because the conditions in the village were not conducive for them; the village lacked medical facilities. Mother had to return to my father at Ibadan with my sister who survived the agony of the relocation to the village; the fear of my father was rested on the early sad event of his mother in her own village Eriki, all which made him to appreciate his wife more.

"Pill all the cassava, cut them and rinse before you soak them for fermentation,"

Grand Ma Loosade said as she walked away to her room.

We were taught how to make local food, from cassava to Gari or Foofoo more like mashed potatoes. We knew, through the system, how to prepare palm oil from the red nuts from the palm tree by crushing the seeds and separating the oil from the shaft. It was a period of love from the extended family; my mother was all about people.

On a fateful day, in the village, as we were playing in the small palm oil-making chamber of one of the locals, an old woman we called "Iya Okan," I mistakenly broke the chamber. The group scattered in various directions. I was left innocently to defend my action.

The Yoruba always addressed people either by their work or children's name. We seldom actually call people by their names. For example, my mother was addressed as Iya Idowu, meaning Idowu's mother. To call her by Iya Bose would be like insulting my senior sister, who was five years older than me.

Iya Okan was a childless old lady who everybody in the village feared because she had a strange way of looking, one eye was turned in. Generally, people made up gossip and stories about her. Some said she must be a witch. Others said she must have used her fallopian tube for something other than what it is meant for, resulting in her childlessness. It was the age of rumor, superstition and ignorance, and the illiteracy of the society did not help the matter.

When Iya Okan found her oil chamber broken, she was enraged and in a very sorrowful and chilling voice she cried out loud,

"Omo Loosade Lofeku mi o", meaning, 'the grandchild of Loosade, who came for vacation, broke my palm oil-making chamber,' in an accent lazed with Egba local dialect. Her voice was very chilling and terrifying, as the villagers wondered who could have dared to cross the old lady.

It was in the middle of the night, when everything was supposed to be quiet, and everybody had settled in to their inner rooms, with bedtime stories being shared by family members. Nights, to us in the village, began when the sun set and it was dark. There were only nighttime noises, the whistles of the night birds, and buzzing insects.

There was no electricity, only mud port, by which palm oil and cotton wool, placed at the edge of the port, became the only means of seeing light, but it was okay. Only those like my grandparents, with children in Lagos, had hurricane lanterns, and in some cases, kerosene lanterns were used. Candle light was not popular then. Besides, it was more economic to use palm oil, which lasted longer than kerosene.

Loosade, my grandmother, had to rebuild the chamber first thing in the morning after she held a meeting with Iya Okan. I was never castigated because no one was allowed to touch her grandson

Idowu, a privilege I enjoyed anytime I was in the village or when my grandmother visited us. The issue was not even discussed as if it never happened. To touch me was to touch any of her gods, I presumed. I loved the freedom and privilege associated with the name.

If I had my way, I would have asked my grandmother to head with me to the school hostel with the emblems and shackles of her gods and show all the wicked school seniors in the hostel or dormitory who used to bully me, so they would know just how powerful she was. But that was just my imagination running wild. I never asked and she never did.

Mother visited me everywhere I lived more than my father. From the time I went to live with Akinde, a teacher, up to the years I resided in the school hostel. She was always concerned about her children. At a time when I was taken to Abeokuta, to attend St. Paul primary school at Igbore, Mr. Akinde was the only teacher capable of handling a troublesome adolescent like me.

He was recommended to my father, who was tired of figuring of what to do with Idowu, his first son. Akinde was a calculative and very good teacher who knew, either by convention or traditional wisdom, how to handle defiant kids. There were three other boys of my age in his home as well, Shina, Tunde, and Bayo, whose parents lived in Lagos.

My parents brought with them a lot of food and money to pay for my care, which I had no access to. I was only given food rich in carbohydrates, leaving the best food for his family. There were sets of rules used in his household. On Saturdays, it was our job to fetch firewood from the village called Ijeun, which we carried on our heads. Unknown to Akinde, we sold some of the wood on the way and kept the money to meet our needs.

"Idowu check the time for me" Mr. Akinde pointed to the wall clock in the living room.

I did not know how to read the hours and minutes of time on the clock. So I kept on starring at the clock on the wall and not knowing what to say or to interpret the long and short of hours and minutes of the big clock...the clock looked like a monster to me.

"Do you need a pair of reading glass to read the time on the clock?" Mr. Akinde thundered from outside. By now everybody was now aware of my inability to read the time on the clock.

"No Sir" I said, blinking my eyes at the clock.

"Then what is the problem?" Mr. Akinde said.

"Em em" I kept on murmuring.

He could not believe I could not read the time on the clock at thirteen years of age, a problem he had to fix immediately. Within two hours of direct one-on-one tutoring, Mr. Akinde had fixed that area of my inadequacy; I could read the time and could also teach others. I was happy with myself.

"Maami, Idowu is washing the dishes" my Sister Bose said, in amazement.

To the surprise of my family every one came to see the new and responsible boy from Akinde's tutelage, with each school vacation I was a changed person. I could help with household activities like cleaning, and checking to see that all things were okay in the house.

"It is only a man there wearing all those funny looking regalia" I said as I pointed to the masquerade trying to educate the people around me.

"Ah the masquerade will cast voodoo on you" Shina said.

"Why and how will he use voodoo," I said in ignorance of the culture of the people of Abeokuta City.

"Masquerade cannot be addressed as a person but representative of the spirits of the dead," Shina further enlightened me.

"But it is still a living person inside the "Eku" "as the costume of the masquerade was often referred to.

"Well just be careful and remember this is Abeokuta not Ibadan," Shina emphasized.

Ibadan City's idea of Masquerade was different from most cities in Nigeria. There was no secrecy on the identity of who was behind the "Eku," it was more like Halloween scene. In Abeokuta it was more of a traditional spiritual war fare. The city was too fetish in spiritual and agonistics outlook than Ibadan. There were lots of cultural and spiritual festivals in which sacrifices were done openly and secretly in the nights. Abeokuta was a scary city in the sixties and seventies.

Years after we left Akinde's place, Shina was the only one I kept in contact with. Bayo died a few years later, and Tunde, who became a medical doctor, relocated to America. But Akinde, reoriented me about life skills and importance of studies; what I learned during my one year stay in Akinde remains the core of my interest in education till today.

Mama never stopped caring about us. The unfaltering love of hers and the greatest of love in her became evident when my brother Biodun, two years younger than me, became ill with polio and sickle cell anemia. He was paralyzed on his right extremities.

When Biodun did offend me, I used to make fun of his situation and he would cry, I never realized how bad it hurt him; it was called kids behavior to tease one another. Mama spent all of her time at University Teaching Hospital at Ibadan taking care of him. The whole family suffered as we all battled to keep Biodun alive.

The family investment went to pay his medical expenses. There was no government support, leaving each family to find their own care whenever and wherever they could find them. There was nothing like medical insurance or medical aid. If your children survived illness it was either luck or divine intervention.

Mama went through difficulties. We all did. I have never seen such a display of love for children in any home as my mother showed. When Biodun eventually died years later, we could see that a part of her was taken away as well. She cried as if he was her only child. But what could one expect from a woman who had gone from ten children to six? The twins had died in a very mysterious way. Five years later, we lost Bimbola my brother to a motor accident. His girlfriend was pregnant at the time, and later had a posthumous daughter my father named Funke.

The first of the twins died at birth, and the second child died in the third month; now two of her sons had died also. She was scared that what happened to my paternal grandmother, who had given birth to thirteen children with only my father surviving, would happen to her as well. Could it be witchcraft or something else? The future might tell.

Biodun's death caused my mother to accept Christianity. She was baptized as Hannah, and joined my father to be an active member of the Roman Catholic Church in our community. She became more committed than most of us, always praying with her rosary in her hand. In fact, I never attended church more than a few times in a year. Her commitment was recognized, and she was decorated with the title of "sweet mother" in the Catholic Church parish in Abeokuta.

When my father died in 2007, the protection I felt toward her was so great that it almost strained the relationship between other members of the family and me. I knew what she had gone through, and my father, who was the protector and custodian of our home, was no longer around. I employed the services of a nursing assistant just to attend to her needs even at the compliant that I was overpaying the nursing assistant; I felt no amount was too much to spend on one's mother.

**Zents Kunle Sowunmi
New York, NY in 2009**

**Zents Kunle Sowunmi inside United Nations Office
New York, NY, 2009**

**Zents Kunle Sowunmi
Ferry to Staten Island, NY, 2009**

Zents Kunle Sowunmi
World Globe in front of UNO, New York, NY 2009

Zents Kunle Sowunmi
President Bill Clinton's first home
Hope, Arkansas, May 2008

**Zents Kunle Sowunmi with senior sister Mrs. Bose Salako
on the day their father was buried, December 2007**

**My Mother
Hannah Bolane Sowunmi nee Onifade**

**My Parents in 1975
Ekotedo, Ibadan**

My father with his nephew Dayo

**Segun Atanda, Biodun Efuniyi, and Zents Kunle Sowunmi
Ibadan Nigeria in 2007**

**Staff members of National Bank of Nigeria, Agodi Branch
Zents Kunle Sowunmi, back row #7 from left**

Final year students, Lisabi Grammar School, Abeokuta 1974
Back Row R to L: Fowler, Sodunke, Parker,
Sopade, Adeyemi and his friend
Kneeling L to R: Lobito Brown, Zents Kunle Sowunmi

PART FIVE

My Early life

Part Five
My Early life

Each day is a chapter in the history of man
Zents Sowunmi

My Early life

❖ ❖ ❖

Nigeria emerged as a country under the Berlin Conference of 1885 in Germany. It was a period in which Chancellor Bismarck, of the newly unified Germany, created almost 34 countries out of the Africa continent and the beginning of the colonization of Africa as well.

After the end of slave trade in 1830 from a struggle led by William Wilberforce, a member of the parliament in Britain, Germany emerged as one of the power brokers of Europe. The need not to escalate war on the former slave routes in Africa among the European former slave dealers and countries in Europe led to the meeting in Berlin in 1885. The meeting was attended by all the powers including France, Germany, Italy, and England.

In Berlin Germany, under the greedy eyes of the world powers, and without consulting the indigenes and their historical and cultural affiliations, Africa continent was selfishly partitioned into countries. Nigeria fell under the control of Great Britain, which was particularly controlled by the UAC (United Africa Company) with corporate offices in Britain. Nigeria, which could have been better off as two countries because of cultural and religious leanings of people around River Niger, or as North and South protectorates, was united in 1914 after the interest of Lord Luggard, the British Governor General.

The first set of military men in West Africa were called British or West African Frontiers, which consisted of soldiers from three other West African countries, including Ghana, Sierra Leone, and Gambia. Liberia, though an English-speaking country, was never part of the British colonies. It emerged from the relocation of the freed slaves from America. Other English-speaking countries, as mentioned earlier, were used by the British to fight during the first and second world wars.

My parents' years in the military were mixed with lots of history and regimented life, which my father eventually found boring. He resigned to join his no-nonsense Uncle Shoyoye at Ile Ife, where he became a produce buyer, which was the business for the rich at that time. Ile Ife was the center of Cocoa trade in West Africa.

All farmers sold their produce to buyers, who in turn sold it to the white man. My Uncle as the buyer was the middle-man, and the career provided an easier way to make money than selling neckties, which was what he had earlier discovered. He had become quite successful, and was willing to share the opportunity with his nephew, my father.

It was a holy alliance; my father managed the office while his uncle took care of the political end of the business. Between the two of them, women played a lot of influence. After years of working together, there was a decline in the Cocoa business and they went their separate ways. My father joined the service of the Western Region in the agricultural department as a clerk, and dedicated 35 years of service to the government, a job that took him to several parts of the Yoruba land.

In between these struggles, he went into importation of electronics from Germany with his high school buddy Chief Farotimi, under a business name Julio-Micho Enterprises. Years of smart business were marred with sharp government activities that led to the collapse of banks in Nigeria. Many lost their investment as many companies went into bankruptcy, including Julio-Micho Enterprise. Papa decided it was over with business for him; he faced his work as a career civil servant.

"When you have a son you must name him Oyekunle," my paternal grandma had said to my father.

Grandma had lost her sight due to years of sadness and prolonged cry as a result of the death of her twelve children; my dad was her only surviving child. She lived with her brother, until her death a couple of years after I was born. She was buried on the site presently used by the Mountain of Mercy Church at Ekotedo, Ibadan.

I was born at Ekotedo, Ibadan on Saturday morning, July 28, and named Oyekunle as requested by my grandmother. Innocent became my baptismal name as a Catholic. I was also named Idowu because I was born after a set of twins in one of the early settlers spots designated for families of those who had something to do with Abeokuta and Ijebus. It was not very uncommon to find most settlers addressing each other as family members or uncles and aunties when in actuality they were not. There were many who addressed my father as such, and it made him happier, since he had lost his biological brothers and sisters. With these extended family members' mentalities, we were like one big family.

Ekotedo held many memories of my youth, and some of the lifelong friends I had made. It was also a place where I had lost much, such as the fire that gutted our home in 1975. A fire, which was caused by the carelessness of our neighbors, had destroyed all my childhood photos. The neighbor had kept gasoline stored behind a door in his house due to shortages. Unaware of this, his wife exposed the gas to naked fire and our neighborhood was set ablaze, five houses in a row.

Most of the landlords were friends or extended families that lived in union and love, and felt it was a waste of time and money to have separate walls. Sometimes, roofs of houses were joined together. It was in the name of love and friendship. How they received government approval for such building plans remained inscrutability, but it was the way houses and homes of that time were arranged. Several decades later, when I visited London, I realized it was the practice to join houses together.

I had gone to work as a teacher in a village 10 miles outside Ibadan. It was my first job. I was so happy, for the first time in my life, to be of significance to the future of the children entrusted in my care.

"Mr. Show I play better than Tunde" Shola said. He was one of my students.

"Let us just wait to see when we come for practice in the evening" I said.

Mr. Show was my aka name with all, including my students. I was the school's coach, and football was my passion. I was happy to take the school to its first competition, though we lost our first game. It however gave the boys a sense of belonging, and the school was never the same again. We won several competitions in our little community before I left.

On the day of the fire, the most important thing to me was the document of my West African School Certificate from my high school, indicating that I had graduated and passed. In 1974 the document was not the original certificate. It was not uncommon to wait for two years before the actual certificate was sent. Losing mine in the fire was the worst thing that could happen to a 19-year-old teenager. I almost went inside to search through the debris of fire for the certificate, as naïve as I was, not accepting that it was only a piece of paper that could be replaced someday. Somebody did go inside the fire.

"Don't let Mr. Pius go inside the fire o?" someone yelled from the crowds of on lookers as the blaze and smoke engulfed the debris of the house.

Mr. Pius, a specialist soldier of Nigeria Army from Benin City and Edo man, who was living in our compound, went inside the burning building. He had hidden his "Udoji" pay arrears (something like stimulus pay), along with his other cash, inside the mattress without informing his wife. It was quite common in those days for a husband to hide his money from his wife, and banking was not reliable.

But Mr. Pius's wife could only salvage a few items within her reach; bed and mattress are not what can be salvaged in a fire accident. Most importantly, she had no knowledge that her husband had money hidden in the mattress. He lost his money and cried like a baby. He blamed his misfortune on coming to work in Yoruba land.

"I wish I had not come to work among the Yoruba o," he lamented in ignorance.

It was also not unheard of to blame your neighbor or friends for any misfortune. In fact, it was often the practice in Africa and the third-world countries in the seventies. They believed that nothing ever happened naturally, somebody must always be responsible. In his case, he blamed the whole Yoruba land for his misfortune; the same community which had blessed him with three children. What an irony of faith.

My father did not own the house we lived in. He rented a three bedroom house situated on Ayorinde Road, in the very heart of Ekotedo, which was noted for the Queen Cinema House, Victoria Hotel, House of Prayer Church, and 16-mouth water pump, which was free to the public. None of the houses in the sixties on our street had built in water pumps. We would fetch water from the 16-mouth water pump located across from Banwo Photo Studio, or the one behind House of Prayer church.

Banwo, the photographer, was a fine looking man, but walked with a limp on his left lower extremity. He was the first man I knew to ride a Vesper or Scooter on our street. The water pump in front of his studio was the social hub for the teenagers to meet in the evenings, with the excuse of fetching water. We watched as the young ladies would carry water away on their heads; sneaking a peek at their butts we whistled in a provocative manner. It was a way to show we were young boys.

Ekotedo had a variety of entertainment going for it. If a parent was not careful, children could be derailed. My mother was determined to make sure we were not. She monitored each one of us like a hen watching over its chicks, protecting them from a hawk attack. She never stopped preaching and motivating us on how we could make our lives better.

We could see people around us destroyed by marijuana, crimes, and prostitution. It was also the community that housed the best entertainment in Ibadan in those days. There was a racetrack for horses, the Scalar and Queen's movie houses, a large golf course and stable for the horses' weekly races along Sabo and Suya, meat vendors, and the rest was like an African mini-version of Las Vegas, Nevada in America. We had lots of clubs like Rainbow, Victoria, and Ladeinde hotels to contend with.

Perhaps one of the funniest things we saw from our place was the lifestyle of our landlord, who had inherited the property from his parents. He was a drunk, and every night he would stay out until midnight or 2 am when most people were fast asleep and snoring. After knocking on the front door several times with no response, he would say in a flat monotonous voice of a drunk,

"Can somebody with sense and who is not drunk open the door for the landlord?" He yelled.

"I have never seen a situation where the tenants would lock the landlord out," He emphasized in the middle of the night.

"Um umm God save me from senseless tenants," he would sometime yell in a crying out loud voice.

By now, the entire household had woken up, tired of his stupid and uncoordinated words, in search of someone at least with "sense" by his recommendation who would open the door for him. Sometimes he would remind us, in the monotonous and irritating voice of a drunk, how he got the property from his father, and sometimes corrected himself or reminded us that the property was originally transferred to his father by his grandmother. Who cares?

However, it was an unwanted mental torturing; same story we were forced to listen to every night. But, it was funny in those days. One of those events in my life I sometimes laugh over. I often wonder if he is still alive.

Papa Tailor, the local tailor, had earned his little spot as a place of gossips for the elderly on our street. His only equipment, his sewing machine which had seen years, and his scissors and ruling tape, were all he had to sustain his livelihood as he criss-crossed his legs in locomotive motion of sewing and still cracking jokes to keep all attentive.

His sewing machine was located almost in front of Papa Ireti's veranda. He never actually took measurements of his clients, he knew them from birth. He would measure the yards of the cloth a customer brought and take a cursory look at his client.

"Come next week it should be ready," he would say.

"Papa Tailor, will you take my measurements?" Sometimes a new customer would ask.

"Never mind I have already," he would say sarcastically.

Most of the promises he made were never kept on time, but all in all, all his clients were satisfied with his work. He was like a friend and father to most of us on our street. A slim man with a penciled-lined mustache, we never knew his wife or children and he never talked about his family; we were all he had. We never knew his actual name so all called him by his profession, "Papa Tailor."

"If you cry again, I will throw this scissors into your mouth," he sometimes threatened kids crying; we knew he was just messing with the kid. He never abused any kid and we grew up almost under the fear that Papa Tailor could discipline us.

By the time I graduated from the high school and during my free time I sometimes, out of boredom, sat at proximity of his trade and could not help but listen to some of his jokes and conversations with Papa Ireti.

Together they formed a perfect union for gossips on women and passersby. Each day Papa Bolaji, a neighbor, was always their talk show. Surprisingly they greeted the man with full respect, but as soon as he turned his back the gossip resumed.

Papa Bolaji was mistakenly arrested for counterfeiting in local currency; it took him years to get out of it. Despite his innocence, the duo of Papa Ireti and Papa Tailor never stopped talking of it. It was the same story I heard over and over again.

Papa Bolaji had himself together; he maintained a mini-zoo for all the wildlife within our community and most of the time some of his prey could not be found at the local zoo. His place was a major scene everyday for foreigners, particularly whites.

Despite the location of his mini-zoo within our community, no hazards were recorded nor any of the animals escaped.

Ekotedo was a small community, not one designed for responsibility but for the fast life, gambling, and prostitution. It was a community where nobody went to bed until midnight, when the last of the crowd from Queen Cinema dispersed. It was a nightmare to get out of that place.

Despite all these shortcomings, it was a community that produced justices like Deinde Soremi and Demola Bakre, professors like Soyode, Adesina and Fafunso, engineers such as late Yomi Adenekan and Segun Oni, and generals and other top military personnel in the Nigeria Army, like the late Colonel Olu Akiode, colonels Ibukun Oyewole and my friend, now retired Col. Segun Atanda, as well as doctors like Toba Elegbe, and Professor Adewuyi, and Tunji Idowu. It was the community that made some richer in knowledge and street smarts. We were able to cross the Rubicon of all childhood problems in our community because our parents, despite their limited education, were determined to see us through.

Childhood responsibilities extended beyond the coffers of each parent. You could be disciplined by any parent on the street. Most acted like keepers of each other's children, a custom that has been removed as the so called western civilization encroached the fabrics of our lives.

As soon I turned 19 years of age, I was tired of listening to any advice. I was ready to be on my own, away from Ekotedo, and ready to live among the upper middle class in a modern area of the city. Mokola and Oremeji were the areas that could fit into my plan, simply because all my hormones were geared toward self-actualization. I was burning with ambition in a variety of fields, as a primary school student of Saint Bridges primary school, Lisabi Grammar School and now as a primary school teacher.

I used to hope that one day I would be privileged to live in areas like Mokola, Oremeji or Bodija, which were considered the cream of the society, and that was what I did when I turned 19. I moved out to live with a friend at Oremeji to be away from all the pressure of the Ekotedo.

My new roommate was a born-again Christian. The term "born-again" was strange to me, as it was to Nicodemus in the Bible. I could not understand how a person could be born again, or join a church that was different from the conventional Catholic, Anglican, Methodist churches, or Aladura white-garment churches that I grew up knowing.

We had a white-garment church in the very house we lived at Ekotedo. We helped the preacher man to play the drums and sometimes added suggestions to the dancing methods used in the church, particularly during the vision revealing exercise.

It was mostly women who would go into a spiritual trance and would reveal visions.

"Thus saith the Lord . . ." they said in prophesy events.

Much like Nostradamus of France had done. In the white-garment church, everybody would be caught up in the spiritual attention waiting his or her turn. One night someone saw a vision that was not favorable in the eyes of my landlord so he closed down the church. That was how we knew the story that led to the establishment of the church. The landlord's sister had returned to the family house after a failed marriage, and her brother had organized the church for her to make a living out of the weekly and daily contributions. But when the weekly visions and trances became too much for the landlord, particularly interfering with his nightly drinking activities, he took side with the booze rather than the Lord. He not only closed the church he rented it to one of his mistresses.

My new roommate was a guy I had met when I was preparing for the General Certificate Advanced Level. We became friends, and both of us were willing to share an apartment, which was common in those days. We went to work and came back home and read. My job as a technical binder with National Archives started making sense to me. It was also a time when I started looking at the opposite sex in a different way.

Lisabi Grammar School which was indeed the first place I had the opportunity to fully integrate with guys from outside my world of Ibadan, Agege and Abeokuta, the only world ever known to me before January of 1970. I was living in the hostel, along with over 150 boys from various communities.

I could remember as if it were yesterday. My mother had accompanied me on my first day in the hostel, most likely to see what the place, as well as the other students, looked like. We often talked about the different kinds of boys in the hostel. Mother took all the Gari more like grits, kuli kuli, adapted from peanuts by the Hausa community, which was usually combined with Gari, sugar to drink, Milo drink and some money for me. It was a joy to be away from home, a kind of freedom and journey toward self-discovery. I made up my mind to enjoy every minute of it, and I did for the next five years.

"You promised me you will face your studies and be a good student" mother said.

"Yes Mama" I said.

We were pioneers of the new dormitory location, and the last to relocate from the old site, at Ijemo Agbadu area of Abeokuta. Moving to the new site within the campus provided a new challenge; scorpions and snakes became our visitors at night. The hostel was in the midst of a big forest. Each one of us was allowed to have a farming plot if we wanted. I did not. I could not stand the sight of wet morning dew, which one encountered on the way to the farm. It had been a thing that disgusted me each time we went for a vacation with my maternal grandfather in the village of Alagbon, very close to Abeokuta.

Along with my new friends, Ebenezer, Lobito, Parker, Emmanuel, and a host of others, farming was not something I enjoyed. Some did, but it was a passion that never developed in us. We played soccer in the evenings, as well as other games children of our age liked to play. A stream, not a river, passes behind the hostel which we often referred to as paradise. It was the place we settled disputes or fights without the knowledge of school authority. It was also where most of the gambling in the school took place among our seniors.

As years went by, nobody was around to counsel us on what to do or how to channel our education towards a fruitful career. We just went to school, passed our grades and moved to the next class. There were no motivational talks from teachers, and if there was one, we never listened except from "Brother Austin" the mathematics instructor. He was closer to most of us than any other teachers in the school.

"Lobito, why are you always reading Bible studies and not mathematics?" Brother Austin said.

Mr. Austin Ugbuegbu our math teacher queried without allowing Lobito to answer, he asked further,

"Are you trying to be a pastor?" He said in his Ibo laced tone of voice. We all started laughing at Lobito, not because he was doing anything wrong but we were all guilty of the same thing. The Bible studies was more like a novel you could read on the bed than mathematics where you have to crack your brain to solve the equations.

Mr. Austin deliberately requested his students to address him as "Brother Austin," and all he wanted was for us to understand his mathematics subject. He believed no class was better than math which was not a friendly subject to most of us. The Bible was all that most of us cared to read. Who cared about Pythagoras' Theorems or simultaneous equations?

Despite the love for the Bible class we were still the bad boys of the hostel. We grew up among older boys who were troublemakers. Their influence was not good on us. Watching them play dice, smoke marijuana, and gamble away their school fees, we could not understand why the Principal could not do anything to stop the activities of our seniors.

They ate our food and left us with crumbs. We were forced to fetch water and even took it to the bathroom for them, made their beds, and were treated like their servants. It was the duty of the junior to serve the seniors; it was like being in the military. If you failed to do this, you would be beaten and harassed by the group. You had to contend with these boys from second to fifth year. Each level of seniority looked forward to the benefits of this feudal system of control over those younger than them. It was not a good thing, it was the way dormitories or hostel life was in the seventies in Nigeria.

The only way to get around this constant punishment and harassment was to adopt one of the seniors as your school father, more like a political godfather. His duty was to ward off any attack from other seniors, but you would have to serve him more. In return, he would introduce you to his girlfriend. She would eventually become your school mother and would take care of you like a son. The whole situation was kind of funny, but it was just that way in the hostel.

David, a tall six-foot boy and one of the meanest of the seniors, became my school father by force. I did not select him, he picked me himself, because nobody wanted him as a school father, and I could not say no. I was rebellious, and he felt he could tame me. He was wrong. Instead of having a father-son relationship, we were enemies from day one. We treated each other with hatred, and because I was skinny and had a smart mouth, he kept me at arm's length.

"I want you to meet Jane who will be your school mother" David said proudly.

Jane was his girlfriend in the school and as his school son Jane automatically became my school mother. David, despite his wickedness, knew how to pick ladies. Jane was very beautiful, had a good set of teeth, smooth and penetrating eyes, and long nose like the Fulani. Her waist and butt moved like a beauty queen. Her eyes were very friendly. Despite my hatred for my school father I kind of liked his choice. I liked my new school mother from day one and she took to me more than I expected. She was a big sister and a mother until she graduated from the school a couple of years later. Jane also on her own had a school daughter, Banke Oyerogba, who by this unconventional system became my school sister.

However, I did not fetch any water for my school father or make his bed as was the custom of the father son relationship in the dormitory; simply because I never even made my own. He beat me on several occasions. He made me wash all of the school's dishes, which I did for several weeks, hoping it was going to be a day or two of punishment. David kept me washing dishes for almost two weeks, until one night I just refused to wash the dishes and there was no clean plate or dish for the whole school to serve dinner. The whole school blamed him. He was mad because of that and kept beating me until I could not take it anymore. I had to do something.

One night as he was sleeping, I almost gouged his eyes out with a compass. That was the day I got my freedom from all the seniors. Both of us were admitted into the hospital. I had stitches on my lips, and he had stitches on his face and parts of his back. From that day on, my schoolmates called me Captain Blood, because my school father had lost a lot of blood. It was also the same bloody fight with another senior Jibodu a year later. We both ended in the hospital and the name Captain Blood got stuck with me for a long time.

My years in high school were not very interesting until the new Vice Principal Oyewole arrived. He changed our ideas about life. He was full of stories, most of them very frightening, discouraging us from sneaking out of the hostel at night. He talked about ghosts and spiritual sacrifices going on at midnight in the cities and junctions. We started imagining things ourselves. He created fear in us.

One of his stories I still remember. He referred to a sickness that defies all medical and traditional approach. The only solution was to transfer the illness from one person to another in order for the sick man to become whole.

"Let me tell you all why you should not go out at midnight" Vice Principal Oyewole said.

"After consulting with an Oracle, the ritual would begin, using a live goat cut open from the midline up. The sick person would stand in the center. The concoction, made of pigeon blood and other unknown objects, was used to bathe him. A foreigner would be handsomely paid to carry the ritual to a designated junction. The person was handsomely paid because that would be the best amount of money he would make in his life, as his entire destiny of success had been washed away. He would be paid up front, and as soon as the ritual was placed at the cross junction he was never to return."

"Griii ouch" Vice Principal Oyewole would clear his throat before continuing the scary story which by then had all of us glued to the edge of our seat. He knew how to add effects to scary events in most of his stories.

"The sick man would continue to have spiritual incantations spoken over him by the native doctor until someone would arrive at the junction and be infected with the sickness. At that moment the sick man would surprisingly ask for water and food, meaning the spiritual prayers and incantation had been accepted by the Oracle."

The sickness had been successfully transferred to the person who arrived at the point of interception; the junction at which the ritual had been placed. It could lead to his or her death. These were stories that explained the sudden illness or death of those who came home from night parties, or traveled at night, and suddenly became sick or dead.

"I hope you can all understand why I said you should not go out of the school Hostel at Mid-night" vice principal said.

"Yes Sir" we all said in chorus like the military men.

The vice principal's terrifying stories of nighttime evil spirits kept us indoors studying. It was no surprise that we all passed our West Africa School certificate with good grades. None of us had the courage to venture out to see if the stories were real or not.

In Abeokuta in the 1970's it was common to find dead bodies and voodoo sacrifices on the junctions of the street of Ijaiye, which made me wonder if those people died after they had witnessed some of the rituals Mr. Oyewole told us. Years later, the vice principal revealed they were all made up stories to keep us in the hostel. It worked on us.

My Work as School Teacher

By the time I graduated from high school in 1974, I had nowhere else to go but return to Ibadan, and teaching was the only job available.

I had registered to teach in a primary school with the local school board. After registration, each day I would wait in line along with others who had applied, as the head teachers of each primary school would pick the next person in line. As the process went, there would be no jumping the line or queue. After seven days of returning to stand in line, it was finally my turn.

The head teacher, a woman in her forties, had seen years of teaching in all areas and had resigned herself to faith of life. She looked tired, worried and desperate. All she wanted was help, and nobody wanted to go to Oganla, the village where her school was located.

The lady next in line refused the job so I jumped at the opportunity. All the paperwork was completed when I realized the distance was too far to take one bus straight to the school. It was too late. I had to ride in the vehicle with traders going to buy food items early in the morning. I did this for several months, until I joined the National Archive, located within the campus of the University of Ibadan.

I was trained as a book binder along with Sunday and Bola, who now lives in the state of New York in America, and Oke, Odejide, Nwanze, and Francis, who was sent for seven-month training in the United Kingdom for Archival Restoration.

Mr. Benedict was our boss. He was a good man who had risen through the ranks as a cleaner until he became the senior technical officer. He had also attended archival book restoration training at Manchester in the UK. He never stopped telling us how beautiful it was over there. Benedict had lived all his life at Ibadan yet he could not speak a single word of the Yoruba language. His children had even passed the language in high school.

"EKUSEo," Mr. Benedict Okarfor said. It was the only Yoruba word he knew laced with his deep Ibo accent; we all loved him. Dan and Francis were also my colleagues at the National Archive, along with these groups of people; I had my first taste of working outside the Yoruba community. It was this environment that removed tribalism and discrimination out of my relations with others.

Department of National Archives was an early morning duty with no second shift. In my case, I had to catch the bus early in the morning to be at work before seven thirty in the morning. I could recollect an event in which a lady was talking and making noise at the same time in the bus, when everybody was in a sober reflection of morning duty. She sat very close to me. I could not bring myself to tell her to bring the conversation to a two person level instead of letting everybody hear the conversation with her friend. She kept on laughing so loud until her dentures fell out her mouth. I started laughing and the other commuters joined me. I guess that silenced her, as she kept quiet until we all alighted from the bus.

We had access to government national supplies, like stock fish and rice, which were distributed to government officials. After spending three years with National Archives, I was ready to move on, which was what I did. But the memory lingers with me.

I joined the National Bank of Nigeria at Ibadan for another year or so before I went back to school, this time to Ogun State Polytechnic to study business administration. I abandoned my ambition to study archeology because I realized archeologists were not properly paid. I had the opportunity to see what they earned due to the nature of my work at the bank.

My trip and eventually permanent residency in America was by accident. I was one of those who never wanted to leave Nigeria. The idea of permanent relocation to a foreign land, after my bitter experience in 1977 with the British Embassy at Ibadan, never crossed my mind.

I was denied a Visa to study transport management at the Center for Business Studies in London. I had met the preliminary requirement for a student visa, and even paid a year's tuition fee, including fourteen months' rent in advance. Still, the British immigration officer denied me a Visa on the grounds that I did not appear to be someone likely to return to Nigeria if given a student visa to Britain. I had appeared too knowledgeable to him about British history, which was exactly what he wrote on the rejection notification.

But, unknown to him, I had just completed the Advanced General Certification in Religious Studies, History, and Economic History. I was very fresh with knowledge; the French Revolution and Industrial Revolution were the areas of history that fascinated me a lot. I read as if possessed. I assimilated all details of information on how Europe went from an agrarian society to an industrial one, after the slave trade and emancipation of the serfs in France. The lives of Louis the XIV, XV, and XVI, of France, German Unifications, and the role played by the Otto Von Bismarck and Napoleonic eras, actually created a deeper role and feeling of what Europe was in my subconscious mind.

I was ready to impress the immigration officer with my knowledge; a fact that made him to conclude that I would never return to Nigeria if given the Visa. He did not give the Visa based on my knowledge. I learned a bitter lesson; never offer more information than what is requested in any situation. Just answer what you are asked, no more and no less.

"I am sorry Mr. Show-me I cannot grant the Visa to Britain" the Immigration officer said.

"Why?" I asked in disbelief of his action.

"I do not think you will come back if I grant you the student visa you want, but you can appeal," he said and gave his reject reasons and steps to follow if I choose to appeal.

I had dreamed of seeing those areas mentioned in the history books I read. I could feel my hand touching the walls of Paris, France, the places where the Versailles treaty was signed, and Waterloo, where Napoleon Bonaparte lost the battle when he tried to invade England. It was all the imagination of my youthful exuberances.

The history of America's War of Independence, and the role of the age of enlightenment, as well as some books and novels on America and Europe, particularly by James Hadley Chase, along with Nick Carter, were the ideals and novelists that made America a dream to most of us who left secondary school in the seventies.

We normally exchanged novels among ourselves on the American way of life, which was portrayed as something close to heaven. We were amazed with the characters such as Albany, the man with his ear to the ground, who was Kola Bello's favorite, Harman Radnize, the rich, ugly, and greedy millionaire, Mark Garland, the retired but often-used CIA agent, and many interesting characters that gave us the impression that the United States of America was everything.

Segun Atanda who became a Colonel in the Nigeria Army later in life wanted to study architecture in the State of Oklahoma. Ilu who died years later preferred Cincinnati and other cities we never knew but liked the way the names sounded. I liked Chicago because it sounded more like bongo drums. Only a few of us later in life made it to America. Others found successes at home. I ended up in Dallas, Texas and New York but visited Chicago years later, the city did not sound like the bongo drums of my youthful thinking it was another rough city like Lagos in Nigeria.

Perhaps, in our minds, the closest thing in our country to America was the environment surrounding the Kingsway store on Lebanon Road at Ibadan; with its paved roads and underground area with the Cocoa Dome, it was the first tallest building in Africa, and one of the legacies of Papa Awolowo when he was Premier of the Western Region in the fifties.

The Kingsway Stores and Cocoa Dome were the center of attention by our own young standards. We could buy our favorite novels; munch some of the memorable meat pies, much like the burgers or sandwiches here in America. We would then retire to Cocoa Dome to see all the girls, only allowing ourselves to gaze at them.

Not that we could not have dated any of them. We were enmeshed with the thought that allowing the idea of dating, or having a relationship with a woman, would mess up our educational goals. That was the belief in those days, especially with the type of upbringing our parents had pumped into our heads.

"You will like the sound bits of your shoes if you face your studies" mother always said, and the motivational messages from all the parents of my friends.

Within our little community, we saw those who had children very young and how they ended up not going back to school. We all dreaded in fear the idea of joining these set of people.

I made lots of friends, immediately after graduation from high school that remained in my circle of trust still today; friends such as Biodun Osomo, Segun Atanda, Kola, and Tunji, Ilu, Paul, Daniel, Olu Akiode, Femi Adewuyi, also called slender boy, Kunle Adegboye, Bode Oyewole, Omoniyi, and Isaac, fondly called Oyinbo, because he was a light-complexioned fine looking man, like a mulatto, and Toba and the late Kayode.

In all, Benjamin and Ramon were two of my primary school friends, but as time went on, I lost contact with these two. I never saw Ramon or Benjamin again. Rotimi Parker whose mother worked with United State Information Services (USIS) at Ibadan, Ebenezer Sopade, Lobito Brown, and Dauda Sokeye were directly my high school buddies, all of us now live in the United States of America.

Most of us enrolled for the General Certification of Education advanced level, with extra Mural Studies Department, organized by the University of Ibadan, while we continued to work to support ourselves. Others went directly to school, particularly Polytechnic at Ibadan, for the same advanced level program.

Kola Bello was one of the few that went to the Polytechnic and later to the University of Ife. I believe he studied English. He was very close to me. We grew up together like the guy next door. His parents were nice and very understanding. His father was very fond of me, calling me by my pet name "Dowu Dowu." He was closer to us, his son's friends, than most of the fathers of others. Kola's mom was very humorous, and together his parents were the happiest couple I knew.

His father consolidated our friendship with the ping-pong table he bought and placed in front of his house, which became a gathering place for us in the evenings. His father was the only man I knew that effectively interacted with his children and his children's friends. He even exchanged novels with us, which reflected on the character of my friend and his brothers.

Kola's friendship remained very golden to me and he knew it. When he came to my father's funeral in December, 2007, he brought his daughter Ope, and from the way she was asking questions and laughing, it was as if she had met a man she heard about for years. I told her that I was just human not a strange person by her imagination. To her, it was like she met a member of the mafia. I guess my friends must have told her different childhood pranks we had together.

Kola's influence rubbed on me greatly regarding my attitude about humility and respect for my elders. I was the typical Idowu, noted for rascality, troublesome, and never afraid. In any form, by Yoruba custom, you were expected to address those who were senior to you in age as someone like a big sister or big brother. In my case, I never followed the rules.

I called everyone by first name, but demanded the seniority treatment from others. My senior sister, Bose, was five years older than me, yet I was always addressing her by her first name, until I met Kola's sister, who was only two years older than us, and Kola was giving respect to her as his senior sister. This made it difficult for me to continue to be "rude" to my own sister. I understood I would have to show the same respect to Kola's sister if I had to continue with our friendship. I did, and it changed my thoughts toward my own "big sister." I became a changed person, and my sister was surprised about this new development. She never asked, and I believed she liked it herself.

Segun Atanda's father, "the old man," as Segun used to call his father, was very cool with us. He appeared to be at peace all the time, one of the attributes I found in my friend Segun. His father treated us with respect, and we all made his place more like a center point. Sometimes we could be up to seventeen, just talking and focusing on academic and social life. We were all from Ekotedo area of Ibadan.

My friend was a calm and collect person, never in a hurry, and always in a happy and organized mood. Nothing worried him. He was always in the right place at the right time. It seemed he never had to struggle too much at anything, unlike the rest of us, and it was said in one African book that he had his faith organized for him by the gods.

He was a friend I could trust with anything. Sometimes, I used to think Segun belonged to the "mafia." He could interact with any group of people without offending anyone, and would expect his friends to do the same, even if it affected the friendship, provided it was the right decision. We enjoyed playing pranks on each other unless you knew us well enough you may fall for them.

"Bro Sege give me something o," A thug name Cafenol once said to Segun.

Cafenol was one of the thugs and street fighters in our community but Segun knew them all, how? I never asked. He gave Cafenol a couple of naira and two sticks of cigarettes and I was wondering how he knew him. But my friend was very close to everyone, the poor and the rich. He was friendly with everyone in our community, but he was full of pranks himself and in most cases no one ever took Segun too serious. He created imaginary stories and events out of any situation.

On one occasion, Segun had visited me at Abeokuta to attend a send off party for Biodun at Ibadan who was departing for London. Bayo my colleague at Ogun state Polytechnic had shown interest to go with us but he was not invited and we could not look him in the face to say no. So we came up with a funny plan. He was invited only if he told his girlfriend, two blocks away, of the trip to Ibadan. He fell for it. By the time he came back we were gone. Bayo never could forget the event for a long time, he felt treated like a kid.

Segun never stopped calling or checking on all his friends, strength of his that, sadly, I do not share.

I found a place to relax between my friendships with Kola and Segun. In fact, my entire circle of friends had a deep connection between these two guys. We loved each other, and the friendship was all that mattered to us. Unknown to them, I could not help but admire their parents. Each one of them represented humility and love. Unknown to them, I did not see much of my father at home, as a career civil servant for the government in another city, he was only home every three weeks, and the company of these two compensated for the missing link.

Biodun Osomo was the third pillar of friendship. His mind was very sharp and he deeply understood people. I met him through Segun Atanda, and he soon became a mirror of affection, respect, love, and understanding, as well as a powerfully trusted buddy. If you ever needed a friend to cry to when you were down, that would have been Biodun who would listen to you and be very understanding. He played much the same role as Meyer Lasky played within the Mafia in the time of Lucky Luciano. Biodun was the linking pin. He represented seventy percent of our circle. If you lost his trust you would have lost seventy percent of the circle. The wives and children trusted his judgments too, and he knew all our children's first, middle, and last names.

Atanda and Biodun became my buddies later than Kola. We could drink, smoke cigarettes, and talk about everything together. Kola would not do all those negative or anti-Christian behaviors. Segun Atanda was more like me, but my love toward Kola never changed. Years later, Kola helped to straighten out my two brothers academically. My friendship with Segun was different. Through Segun, I met a group of boys from P & T Training School in Oshodi, Lagos; like Prince Tolu Onisile and Kayode Makun, Sofela, and a host of others. As we advanced in age we all made new friends but never broke that link with one another. Segun found his life expectations in the Army, Kola as a principal in a secondary school, and I found mine as a therapist and businessman in the United States of America. Kayode Makun also relocated to Texas before moving to Chicago and then Detroit, Michigan, USA.

Along with 200 new other students, I became a pioneer of the new school that had come as a result of disagreement between Ogun State Government and Oyo State over the funding of the Polytechnic at Ibadan. Ogun State went ahead and established a new State Polytechnic in 1978 from the school ground of a secondary school in Abeokuta.

We started the student union, along with the late Sola Alakija and Kehinde Sokeye, Popoola, Akinbode, Mould, and a host of others. However Sola and Kehinde later became political rivals, with me in the center of their political antics and manipulations. I was called Zik by all in the School, due to my ability to get along with both of them despite their rivalry. Zik was the name of the first Nigeria ceremonial President Dr. Nnamdi Azikwe, and he was notorious for understanding the politics of the North and West in Nigeria in the sixties. Both remained my friends until Sola died of a heart attack and brain tumor in 1982 and Kenny died of the same problem 12 years later.

Sola served as the student welfare secretary and had fought for the purchase of an ambulance for the school. Unknown to all, he would be the first dead person to use it. We took his corpse in the ambulance, and his death, still today, remains a mystery to me. We had studied overnight in my room before we ran into a troubled academic water of understanding some principles of cost accounting, and decided to reconvene in my apartment later in the evening. Forty days before the date of examination, Sola's senior brother had died in a motor accident, and that also had affected his concentration, which made me more his pillar of support and the shoulder he cried on.

We were preparing for the end-of-term examination in cost accounting. It was the most difficult of the classes. Sola was not that good in cost accounting. I was just an average person in the same subject myself. In fact, Sola hated figures. He barely scaled through most classes involving figures. We became friends through a mutual respect for each other, along with stories he had heard about me from a childhood friend of his, Lobito, who had attended Lisabi Grammar School with me. From day one, we clicked like a chemical solution and were inseparable. Politics and social life was natural for both of us. He was the son of the Nigerian first Minister of Health, Dr. Alakija, in the First Republic.

Sola did not show up as arranged. He knew where I kept the key to my apartment. I had left his favorite drink in my refrigerator and gone out to see a couple of friends until late in the night. I gave up on him when he did not show up and planned to see him in the morning before the test. That night, I had a dream in which I was in the classroom getting ready for the test along with the other students. Sola was resting his back against a white Peugeot car parked outside the test center; "Show," he said, which was the name he called me.

"Come in and take the test," I said.

"Show, I told you I have all the answers here in my folder" Sola said.

"I know, but you will have to come into the examination Hall and write it down, to get credit for all your knowledge," I emphasized.

"You don't understand," He said. He walked away from the test center. I kept on calling him to come back, but he never did in my dream. I woke up.

I did not think anything of the dream until I got to his apartment the following morning, only to be told that Sola died six hours after he left my apartment. I guess the dream was a way to say goodbye to his friend. It was June 24, 1981 on his 24th birthday.

His mother had sent food and drinks from Lagos to commemorate his birthday, and along with three other friends, Pius Aloha, Yemi Oyadina, and Lawal, they ate the food and drank the wine drinks from his mother until Sola complained of dizziness. As was the local custom, he was asked to rub his face with the juice of his armpit to reduce the dizziness, which he did until blood started gushing out his nose. He was rushed to the hospital, and died fifteen minutes later at exactly 3:15 pm of heart attack and brain tumor or damaged artery.

All the closest friends of Sola that ate the same food were tested for food poison. The test was negative, but he never stopped appearing to some of us in dreams. At one time we were all afraid, and decided to share the same room in prayers, when it dawned on us that he wanted us all to join him wherever he was.

On the eve of the night before he was buried, I saw him again in my dream. He had a bandage around his head towards his frontal lobe. It was soaked in blood on the right side. He told me he was not dead, all he had was a wound on his forehead. In my dream, I told him that could not be so, and he wanted me to place my hand on his head to feel it. I refused, and somehow I woke up and realized it was only a dream.

I went to see my mother and explained the whole story, including the dreams, to her. She did what most mothers of her generation among the Yoruba tribe would do; she marked my face with two incisions on both cheeks to prevent me from seeing strange things again. It was indeed a form of placebo medication treatment, I found out later in years, but I still carry the marks on my face today. I never saw Sola again in my dreams.

Sola's casket was displayed for public viewing in the school hall. When he was about to be interned, I never stopped thinking if he was only in the state of coma, and if I should ask the casket to be opened to see if he had regained consciousness. I never asked.

What will people around say or will they listen to me? Will I be another Jesus or just an insane and infatuated friend? I could not bring myself to say anything at his funeral. All I did was cry; it was like a part of me went away.

I never actively participated in Student Union politics again, but remained more like a godfather.

I was in the moaning mood for thirty days in black dress, wondering what could have taken away the life of a promising character for future national politics. Surprisingly and strangely, forty days later, Sola's baby brother in Lagos also died in a similar way. Could it be witchcraft or the effect of the polygamous life of his late father? We never knew and we never asked. When it comes to any suspicion of witchcraft, everybody seems to take the back seat; else "they" may come for you also.

It was often common to refer to a story in which the misfortune of the city noted had been caused by the works of witches, and the mother to the King of the city was assumed to be the leader of the witches. The whole community decided to confront the King and his mother in the open. The leader of the group was to start the conversation and in unison with the whole community, must conclude with a shout, "Your mother is a witch."

The leader of the group presented his case and concerns to the King in the open Town Hall meeting as planned. As he got to the time when the whole community was to respond with, "Your mother is a witch," all kept quiet. Since he could not say the words solely by himself, to save himself from the situation he repeated the same statement and again nobody responded with the planned statement of the King's mother was a witch. To save his head he concluded with, "Your mother was very Blessed with good health," instead of using the word witchcraft.

Such was the fear in our community of witchcraft. We never wanted to find out more about the death of Sola. Even if we ever thought of it we kept it to ourselves in fear of witchcraft repercussions. I never stopped wondering if Sola regained consciousness before he was buried.

Kehinde Sokeye, his political rival and a mutual friend to both of us, later, in the academic and political program, became the President of Ogun State students for the whole country to compensate for his loss of the Student Union Presidency in 1981. Our friendship remained stronger, and his wife could not understand how we could disagree without being disagreeable. After each fierce argument we used to end the day on a friendly note. No argument lasted more than necessary.

Twelve years after we graduated, Kehinde died of a heart attack. He was survived by his good wife and three boys. The news of his death filtered to me in my new country, America, through a friend, Akinbode, in Austin, Texas. It shook me like a bullet, because I knew his ambition was to run for the elected office of Governor of our state. He worked tirelessly for it building bridges. Each time we talked, it was all about realization of the goal, and his love for his sons, particularly Femi.

Graduation from Ogun State Polytechnic in 1983, with a Higher National Diploma in Business Administration, along with Bayo, the late Kehinde, Isaac, Kamaru, Lakabo, Patrick Ilo, Sola O., Sola Bakare who became Marketing Manager for Eleganza industries in Lagos, Kunle, and Sola G., was an event that gave each one of us hope. We went through years pioneering toward success, between accreditation and recommendation, and we were determined to place our new school on the world map. Two students did not graduate with us, due to deaths, and another four left the program halfway through to pursue another dream, like Kunle Osota who later became the Chief Land Officer for the State of Ogun in Nigeria.

It was not long before I, along with Mrs. Obey who graduated with HND in Accountancy, became the first of the old students to graduate from the University of Ibadan with a Masters Degree in Business Administration. Kunle Akiode followed suit two years later, with a Masters in Banking and Finance, along with Institute of Chartered Accountant (ICAN). He became a published author within two years of graduating from Polytechnic. Lakabo became an international businessman, with offices in America, Britain, and Nigeria, and Kunle Amosu became a Senator in Nigeria, with a host of achievements that could not all be mentioned due to space. Each one of us was doing his or her part in planting the sole of our school on the threshold of history.

It was a mandatory exercise for graduates of universities, Polytechnic, and other colleges, to go through the one-year National Youth Service Program. It was not uncommon for the citizens to resort to arson and massive killing if things did not go well in the general election in Nigeria. The whole country was disillusioned with the civilian government of President Shagari; corruption was a way of life. People had lost their jobs, and the trust in leadership had failed. I was not ready to venture beyond the areas of my tribe for any national assignment in view of the coming national election in 1983.

As was the custom, my sister knew someone who knew someone who had worked with me at National Achieves at Ibadan in the seventies. A big civil servant deployed to work at NYSC in Lagos, he influenced my posting and Lagos State became my post along with my buddy Bayo.

I was posted to the National Library in Lagos, the beginning of a new experience for me. I made new friends from other institutions, but the group from the University of Lagos interested me. They often talked about the "Okafor theory". Unknown to me, it was not a decent theory, at least not for this publication; it was a "man's thing" about having relations again with a lady after a breakup. My roommate was a medical doctor on internship. He was a product of the University of Lagos, and we met through a common friend a Navy officer and Medical Doctor, Toba Elegbe who had been given the apartment, but decided to let us have it because he had another one in Lagos.

The year moved faster than expected. As expected the federal elections had been rigged by the incumbent President Shagari government again. As expected, it led to a military takeover of the federal government on New Year's Eve of 1984, which made the economy to go south. We all returned in fear to our states of origin to look for jobs, as none were available to non-indigenes of Lagos unless they were well connected. I was not.

Teaching was the only option my state could offer. Kobape High School, a few miles away from Abeokuta, was my first posting. I taught accounting, commerce, and business studies along with Femi Adebajo, Taiwo Abati, Bisi Adekitan, and a host of other teachers. We put in our best, and within two years we had two school principals, but it never satisfied my expectations. With a background in Business Administration, coupled with professional qualifications of the Institute of Purchasing and Supply Management and Chartered Institute of Marketing, teaching could not meet my life and academic expectations.

A year after I left Ogun State Polytechnic in 1983, I was on my own, with no family support to climb the ladder of opportunity in a society that needed family connections to get good jobs or business opportunities. I was determined to soldier on with whatever fate had for me, but it was tough, as all roads to success were closed to me. A teaching job was the only route in my state after graduation. I was already a father with my first daughter, she was about a year old; raising a family was a tougher job than I had expected.

Abidemi was a special kid from birth, very demanding in her needs. She needed two feeding bottles at the same time before she could eat, and all she wanted was a special brand of baby food, which was then difficult to get. Each time we switched to what was available and used by other kids, her system rejected it.

Like the prodigal son in the Bible, except that I did not actually ask for any inheritance like the Biblical story, I went to my father and asked if he had any family connections to help in finding a good job.

"Papa, who can I ask to help me find a job; I am tired of being a teacher in a village high school," I asked my father.

He gave two family links, the Chairman of Societe Generale Bank in Lagos, Chief Kotoye, a relative on his paternal side, and Engineer Ayo Obaseki on his maternal side.

"Talk to your Uncle Ayo Obaseki," he said.

Ayo Obaseki was the National Electric Power Authority Director posted to Abeokuta, my hometown in the eighties. His mother was my father's aunt and, honestly, the connection was so interwoven that I could not trace the lineage. All I knew was when he was in high school, he used to spend his school vacation with my father.

He was a time-conscious person, and I was late to his office the first time I was to see him. Uncle Obaseki sent me back and I had to reschedule the appointment. He was a slim guy of almost six feet tall, a fast talker and very much in control of his figure; a deliberate workout system that took his life on the gulf field years later.

Uncle Obaseki talked to the Ogun State Commissioner for Finance who directed me to the new Ogun State government joint project with Euro Technical of Milan Italy, Gateway Pharmaceutical Company (GPC). I became the Administrative/Project Secretary of a project that was an immediate clash of interest between the two major ethnics group in the state. Unknown to my uncle and the rest of the company, I had sent several applications that were never acknowledged. To enter or advance in the business community in the eighties was based on family connections.

My schedule was to liaise with the Central Bank of Nigeria Import department on "Form M" processing on behalf of the State Government, and Federal Ministry of Trade, since the project was a joint venture between Italy and Ogun State government.

Gateway Pharmaceutical Company turned out to be a nightmare for a young graduate, rather than a learning platform for career growth. It was a ruthless ground for corruption, and nepotism, and blatant disregard for rule of law. The management was openly stealing from the system and the government of Ogun State was in support of everything. At a stage, I was wondering if something was not wrong with me for not joining them.

In between, I never gave up on my paternal side in my job search. Chief Kotoye was having problems with another Shareholder of **Societe Generale Bank**, and it became national sensational news for the media. Hiring a distant nephew was not on his priority in the midst of management crises. After traveling several times to see him at his Ikoyi Lagos office without any concrete thing to hold on to, I gave up seeking a position through him.

He lost his position as the Chairman of the Bank due to boardroom politics and greed on both parts. My visitation cemented my friendship with his first son who was my age mate. Lack of communication in Nigeria in the eighties was not enough to keep contact, so the son and I lost contact.

It dawned on me as time went on that if I had to survive, I have to fend for myself; I have to be a little bit selfish with life, be ruthless in my decisions, and never to look back on family for help, but to take my fate in my hands. I did just that.

I wanted more in life than what the Higher National Diploma in Business Administration Certificate could offer. I buried my head in serious academic pursuit. I was ready to seek salvation through studies, rather than corruption of mind and soul. Two years after graduation from Polytechnic, I had completed the professional certifications of the Chartered Institute of Purchasing and Supply Management and that of Chartered Institutes of Marketing of Great Britain through correspondence studies. My friend Biodun Osomo in London was one of the few that believed in me, probably because our backgrounds were similar and he appreciated my role when he was to travel out of the country.

I was ready for the next step of my plan. In 1987, four years after leaving Polytechnic, I became one of the two ex-students of Ogun State Polytechnic to be admitted into the University of Ibadan for the Master's Degree in Business Administration. I could not secure any government funding for the program or from the Company; all I got was study leave without pay.

The eighteen-month MBA program was hectic for me; I had no money for extracurricular activities. I turned my Volkswagen Beetle car to a cab between Abeokuta and Ibadan to pay most of my needs and the support of my landlord, the late Yomi Adenekan who was Director of Works in my State, helped to keep my apartment.

"Pay me all your rents after graduation," he said.

"Thank you Egbon," I said in total appreciation.

He had seen the way I was struggling and shuttling between Ibadan and Abeokuta during the program.

The day of graduation from the University of Ibadan was a mixed blessing for me; I was broke, totally broke.

I could not even attend my own graduation; I could not afford the academic gown and other required payment for the events. I collected my certificate and went into the only Catholic Church on the campus and laid it on the altar and talked directly to God.

"Please God get me out of this hell," I prayed out loudly.

I made the effort to re-enroll into the University again for a law degree but was told two paper qualifications were enough.

"Mr. Sowunmi, the University does not encourage career students and besides, we think you have stayed long enough in school to know what you want," the Academic Registrar said while turning down my application.

"Give others a chance to earn a degree," he said further.

I walked out of his office deflated; that was years ago.

GPC started in Abeokuta before it moved to its permanent site in Ijebu Ode. GPC was designed and conceived to make use of the six production lines to produce pharmaceutical drugs, which would have taken care of the free medical treatment program under the leadership of the Unity Party of Nigeria, which lost the federal elections in 1983. The company became an elephant project, much to the disheartening of the state government and the Italian Partner Eurotechnica of Milan Italy.

The politics of ethnic rivalry of the Egba and Ijebus in my state was too much for me at GPC. Each ethnic group within the state was ready to sacrifice quality to substandard levels. I was torn between loyalty to the group and becoming part of the corruption in the state. I was naïve to the system.

I was a deep product of a Christian background, based on the Ten Commandments as pumped into my head by my parents, from the time I was an altar boy in the Catholic Church of St. Gabriel at Ibadan and Lisabi Grammar School.

"Thou shall not steal."

It was the most cherished one of the Ten Commandments. I could not understand why a man placed in control of a big project by the government would be stealing, or diverting the resources meant for the project for his personal use. Nobody taught us this process in the business school. The politics of stealing and getting away with it was strange to me.

I was having problems with my boss and his accountant. Some of the politics or meetings were done behind my back, and some of the decisions I made in the best interest of the company and staff made me appear not to be a team player. The workers were not paid overtime, and I was more on the side of the workers than the management. I guess as a former student union leader, it was difficult for me to take side with the management.

I could not understand. I was searching for reasons in the wrong direction and from corrupt people all over the state; some even told me to be understanding of the system, like my teacher in the High School. I started hearing stories of imaginary deaths or insanity that had happened to people who had tried to expose the situation in the past. I could not find the solution in the system of support around me. Voodoo was used against me at work, and my office tables started being sprayed with unknown powders.

There were times, the security guards told me, that some of the senior staff had come into my office at night. I started asking the opinion of leaders within my community about how things could be changed or approached. My options were not good. It seemed I would have to either join them or become a member of secret society, which I was not ready for. As imperfect as my Christianity was, secret society was not an option for me, I still trusted the Lord Jesus except I could not see him physically to fight my emotional and brain torturing battles.

I did not find a solution until I went on study leave for the MBA program at the University of Ibadan in 1987. When I returned, in March of 1989, the politics had become even worse. The friendly GPC Board of Directors had been dissolved, and replaced by men appointed by the Military Governor Lawal.

The new military president known as IBB had visited the state and the gigantic pharmaceutical company. He was impressed with what he saw on the ground and understood the state needed assistant to complete the project. Without proper accounting discussion like all Military government, he promised the state a sum of 100 million naira to complete the project.

The Military Governor Lawal planned to divert the 100 million naira promised by the federal government, which under the leadership of the GPC Chairman Professor Bamigbose a "born gain" might not have been possible. The Governor, in his wisdom or otherwise, dissolved the Board and appointed members of his cabinet as new board members.

Stealing became openly legalized. Cables and industrial equipment were openly removed and stolen. It was a sorry situation when I returned from eighteen months' study leave. Tears flooded my eyes. The project originally was meant to hire over 500 university graduates from all fields. Everything was being left unattended too, and chances of ever seeing completion looked remote. I started planning my exit.

I had spent three months of industrial quality time with Pfizer, a very big pharmaceutical company in Lagos. I was thinking Ogun State could outsmart the United States of America corporate based pharmaceutical company in Lagos after I saw the industrial machines they had, and that they were making millions of naira in profit. To be fair to Pfizer, they had less than ten percent of what we had in equipment at Gateway Pharmaceutical Company, but the management was solid and focused, which was what was lacking in my company.

"There is a big lizard on the table," my daughter, Stella said.

I asked her to get a pen from the table in my bedroom. I have always been an early riser, usually up between 4 and 5 am. In most cases, I tried to influence everyone in my household to do the same, and my children had to live with this aspect of their father. We never slept till 6 am. Even on weekends.

I saw what my daughter called a big lizard myself. It was not just a lizard, but a big alligator reptile, with its tongue splitting out like a dragon. It had climbed up the blind in my room. It dawned on me that this was not an ordinary event in an apartment with a screen on the windows, no bushes nearby, or in a second-story apartment.

How the reptile got there, or entered my bedroom, was difficult for me to comprehend. I got the members of my household out and called the security guard in the compound. He was an old man in his seventies with some visible and countable teeth in his mouth, like many illiterates of his type. Due to the nature of his profession, he put a leaf between his lips and rendered some incantation before commanding and killing the reptile. He requested that I should be careful of imaginary and spiritual enemies. He cut the head of the reptile and wanted to make a fetish food of it for me so that all my enemies would die.

"Papa, I appreciate your offer but my Christian background makes it difficult for me to do that except to pray for whoever was responsible" I said.

"This is the problem with you Christians. Why and how you can be talking of prayer and mercy for anyone who planned to kill you?" He said before he left.

Niger Cedar Industries

I was deeply touched and lost interest in my job for the State of Ogun in Nigeria. I never stopped being amazed at what people could do to attain diabolical objectives towards perpetrating corruption; human lives meant nothing to them. I decided to move on, and started applying for jobs outside my state.

Kayode Akinbode was my confidant in most family and work related matters because we shared similar family situations; a very kind hearted friend with a fantastic wife, with a very strong Christian principle. He was a prayer warrior. I was not, and I was much more comfortable in saying the grace than total long mouth twisting prayers and speaking in tongues. Kayode would pray before everything, food, sleep, outings, before touching the ignition of his car. I remember being with him and a friend and we were served the food, I just started eating until Kayode requested me to pray for everybody before we could eat. I had my mouth full already. I was embarrassed but I had to pray in such a way to accommodate my failure.

"Lord we thank you for this food which my prayer is meeting along the way."

"Amen" they all said with laughter.

It was not long before I was appointed as Marketing and Sales Manager for Niger Cedar Industries, situated at the Isheri Ojudu border town between Lagos and Ogun States. I was glad to move on from GPC and never stopped wondering if they all realized that they were in bondage of Satan in their diabolical situation.

I was able to fully interact with the completely Igbo-dominated tribe of the business owner. I was the first Yoruba man to be marketing manager in the history of the company. Unknown to them, my experience with the Department National Archives at Ibadan helped me to integrate with the staff of the company quickly.

A staff could be hired by the company for different reasons, not necessarily known to the hired staff. I was able to figure this out because the company distributors in Lagos were all of the Igbos tribe, and the new general manager wanted that to change. The new marketing manager being from outside the Igbo tribe would be ideal. It worked for both of us.

Sunny Elijah, the chief accountant, and the production manager, Egesi, became very close to me. We worked like a team. In the evenings, Elijah and I met regularly, at a club owned by his friend "De Cool," for our regular "Ishi e wu", goat head pepper soup and beer before leaving for Abeokuta or Sango Otta to be with our families. I did not live in Lagos because it was cheaper and cost effective to do so within a 45 mile radius. There was no need for it.

We turned the company around and sales tripled. The management was happy with our job, and the company regained its leadership position in the wood-finishing and adhesive industries. We were neck-and-neck in competition with Berger Paints, Dunlop Industries, IPWA, Premier Paint, and Ereke Industries. My activities led to my election as the publicity secretary for the Adhesives Manufacturers Association of Nigeria. The company started exportation to Ghana, Gabon, and other West African countries.

I was an aggressive marketing manager. I went after big accounts dominated by Berger Paints and Dunlop Industries, offered mouth watering discounts in all forms to buyers. We delivered directly to the users, and when the buyer was not playing ball, we'd sometimes leave some products free for them. We kept on with the cold calls until someone listened. Sometimes we looked for friends of the King of the city or the person in charge of purchases, or buyers of the company who could make a decision. We cut a lot of deals to get contracts. It was fun doing business in Lagos with people who had polished minds, unlike those in Ogun State.

The Annual Association event of the Adhesive Manufacturers of Nigeria was given adequate publicity by all the major newspapers. **Guardian News** in Nigeria did a preview on the association in its supplementary edition and my efforts for the association were commended. I was beginning to look like a voice in the industry. I started receiving invitations to attend functions on behalf of my company, as well as that of the Association.

During the Nigeria Music Awards hosted at the National Theater, when Shina Peters and Alhaji Ayinla Kolington were recognized for their exploits in both Juju and Fuji music, respectively. I was one of the invited guests. My career was looking good to me, but it was not long before things started changing otherwise.

Rockwood Industries Otta

Poach was a term used when you steal a staff member from another company, and I was poached from my company to be with Rockwood Industries as Commercial Manager. With all the paraphernalia of the good office, and at a time when Racer Dee Wood was the newest car on Nigeria roads, initially everything looked rosy. Within three months of joining the company as commercial manager, the company failed to secure the anticipated World Bank loan it was processing and I was laid off. For the first time in my life, I was out of a job. Yes I was.

It was then the phrase, *recession and depression*, as defined by the former and late President of the United States, Republican Ronald Regan, made sense to me. He had said, in one of his often comical speeches, the difference between depression and recession, "Recession is when your neighbor loses his job and depression is when you lose yours." I guess I was now in depression.

Every disappointment led to a hidden blessing. I started thinking in word and decided to write a feasibility study toward my own company. Two months later I was ready and in search of finance for a manufacturing company in adhesives, polish and paint. The company started with my little savings and I was glad to name the product "New World." I continued to source funding toward expansion, which made me to contact my old schoolmates from the University of Ibadan who were top executives with the banks in Nigeria.

PART SIX

The Glass as Mirror of Life

Part Six
The Glass as Mirror of Life

*To find a new Lead actor for a
new movie you must first write the script*

-Joe Scarborough
MSNBC

The Glass as Mirror of Life

❖ ❖ ❖

We, the Yoruba, regard our fathers as mirrors and mothers as jewels and even without the knowledge of the science of DNA, it is our belief that a child must look like his father in words and deeds, and if not, something is missing and the mother's faithfulness is questionable.

I was a carbon copy of my father, so were all my brothers. What I lacked of him was patience, which must have inherited from my mother, who had no patience and was undeniably the matriarch of the home.

When Papa rose to the position of Executive Officer as a civil servant, he was given a loan by the government to purchase a car. He bought a brand new Volkswagen Beetle. It was the best thing that ever happened to him, because having a car in Nigeria, as in any many other third world countries, was not only a luxury, but also an additional freedom: freedom to come and freedom to go. It was a joy to detail and clean one's father's car in the open space of our street, an additional demonstration of the family's prosperity.

My friend Segun Atanda's father bought a very popular green car with a brand name "Avenger" and so I asked him for technical advice as to how to detail cars. He seemed to be an expert in those days and always telling us his friends how he was going 'to inherit the car as soon as he turned 21".

"That will be my car when I turn 21 on my birthday" Segun always reminded us.

"How do you know the "Old Man will give it to you? I asked.

"I heard him telling my mother" Segun lied.

"And how come he did not give your senior brother the car" I asked further.

Segun laughed and he knew he was playing his pranks again.

We never took Segun too serious as he could make up tales and, if you were not used to his pranks you would be taken for a ride. As for me, the way my father cherished his new car I was not sure if I could say the same, but the joy of partaking in cleaning it like my friends did to their fathers' cars was good enough for me.

My father took all of us, in the car, to the church and to visit longtime friends and relatives. Unfortunately he only had the car for less than eight months before it was stolen in front of our home at Ekotedo, Ibadan.

"Where is my car?" My father said early in the morning.

"It should be outside, I saw it last night!" someone said.

The day it was stolen was an ugly day in the life of the family; we were looking for the car as if it was a box of matches. We searched everywhere, but after our long search, which included tracing the line of the tire to the major road before it faded away, and a negative police report, my father gave up on the search. He was paid his claims by the insurance; he used the proceeds to start a new property in his hometown. He never bought another car. I could see the sadness in his eyes; personally, I wept myself, not because of the loss of the car, but to see my father's joy of owning that car taken away by the thieves, after years of laboring for the government as a civil servant.

Having a home of your own could bring peace of mind more than having a car, though it was better to have both. But between the two, a home should come first; not a single worry from unreasonable landlords. God knows we had faced many of them in the past, particularly at Ibadan. Having a home provided freedom, freedom to do anything we wanted without limitations and that was our joy when my parents finally moved into the new, eight-bedroom house in our hometown of Abeokuta.

It was not fully completed; only the first four bedrooms were ready, which was okay for the Old Man and my mother. I had moved out at the age of nineteen, and only two of my siblings were still living with my parents. Every day, along with my other brothers and sisters, we visited our parents. The sadness in my father's eyes was still there, even though he enjoyed his new surroundings as a home owner.

We were free to have family meetings and we became much more united. Visits to our parents occurred more and more often and were always joyous moments. The home brought our family closer, more than the car ever did. Perhaps the loss of the car was a blessing in disguise from the father in heaven.

PART SEVEN

Old Man Finally Left Us

Part Seven
Old Man Finally Left Us

"Death You Cannot Take My Joy"
-Zents Sowunmi

Old Man Finally Left Us

❖ ❖ ❖

My previous trip experience to Nigeria in 2003 was not what I had expected. Visiting Africa, after seven years in America, was not everything I had looked forward to. I had dreamed many dreams of what Africa would look like. I had imagined Nigeria would be growing along with the type of development I had seen in the western world, but I was disappointed and totally disillusioned from the moment I could see daylight in Lagos from the sky.

Before the airplane landed, we had to circle around Lagos owing to some logistics problem. In the background was the Ogun River, which spread more than ten times away from Ikeja to the Lagos Ibadan Express road. We could see with a bird's eye view what type of landscaping we had; it was brownish, unpaved road. The grass on the airport field was not properly trimmed, and it was burnt. We alighted from the airplane into the beautiful walkway of the airport, built in 1977 for the Festival of Arts and Culture, which Nigeria hosted later in that year. The Festival exposed the country and its riches and beauty to the black nations.

I had missed my children a lot, but never stopped communicating with them on the phone or in writing. When email became fashionable, it even made things better. The last time I saw them, they were 12 and 9 years old respectively; I was wondering what Asero would look like in Abeokuta the rock city.

After months of savings for the air ticket to travel, I met Pete Ade, the owner of Africa Travel, an agency in Dallas, Texas. He explained the new "wonder flights" operating directly to Lagos from Atlanta, Georgia, by World Airways. I should have known better. Direct flights from Nigeria to America had been cancelled in the past due to many reasons from politics to corruption and this new development was a relief to most Nigerians that had to travel through Europe before coming to the United States of America.

On December 19th, 2003, I arrived at the Atlanta Airport from DFW in Dallas, Texas with several hundred Nigerians. The airport was equally as busy as DFW in Dallas, but not as beautiful. We pride ourselves in Texas for having one of the best airports in the world, and it is true. Texas is a state that automatically makes you feel like a proud person, and is a feeling rarely found in other states. Subconsciously, somehow you think of yourself more highly than others and, in my opinion, it takes a lot of effort to see a humble Texan. Why is that? The State has over 40 percent of United States of America exports, over 500 fortune companies most of them with corporate offices in Dallas. In Texas we do not pay state tax, unlike most other states in the country. Here in Texas we have the Cowboys, a football team, better known as the nations team, the Mavericks, the Texas Rangers, Houston Rockets, San Antonio Spurs, and the state was often described as "everything is big in Texas", with Dallas as the number one trading City to China. In the USA the sport football should not be confused with soccer; football in America is like the game Rugby, played in most countries of the world. Thus, I was looking for the same Dallas standard in Atlanta, which, unfortunately I did not find. To me Atlanta's Airport looked like Love Field Airport, a municipal and local airport located in Dallas, Texas.

I should have suspected something negative, as no serious arrangements were made by the World Airline to accommodate the increasing number of passengers, who came from all over the country to try this new direct flight from Atlanta to Lagos. It was like Nigerians going home were ready to ship away anything that could be seen on America streets. My two big bags looked more like those belonging to someone not prepared for the journey. Boxes were stacked on top of each other and additional fees were paid for excess luggage. I was wondering if I should add more to my luggage.

I sat down in a bed view corner to see all the happenings on the tarmac and around. Passengers were not following the rule of first come first serve on the line. Some cut the queue and they pretended as if they were just talking, and then cleverly, without shame joined the line. It was that which made me uncomfortable, as the line was getting longer through this deception.

"You cannot jump the line while others followed the rules" I charged a man who just jumped the queue.

I was expecting support from fellow passengers on the queue to address the anti-social behavior. They all just pretended as if everything was okay and I was the odd man, after years in a first world country one would expect something better but it was not.

Far away, in downtown Dallas Texas, I could remember reading an inscription on the ground at the West End Bus station. It read, "This city was established by John Bryan in 1841." That was nine years after Abeokuta a City of the Egbas in Ogun State, my very hometown, migrated from Ibadan. I was going to take a cursory and sober look at the development that happened during my seven years of living in Dallas, and the eight years since I left Abeokuta. Unfortunately, I was not prepared for what I saw.

After a six hour delay, the chartered World Airplane finally took off from Atlanta Airport on what was supposed to be a direct flight to Lagos. It stopped in Cape Verde Island for almost 2 hours. Nobody told us why, but we heard that the plane was refueling. The food was just average not like the KLM, British Airways or Lufthansa I had experienced in the past. Just average, including the attitude of the air hostess, but it was okay to fly home directly looking at the beautiful ocean pointing directly to Africa instead of Europe. I could see the joy on the faces of all Nigerians, as we seated and talked in loud Nigerian tones without any white faces around. Going home was a joy to most.

I had enough time to reflect on the past. I thought of the events that had happened in Dallas in the past seven years, in terms of the various infrastructures, the extension of Highway 75 which was opened in 1997 was one of the best in the world, running from a small city in Oklahoma to downtown Dallas. The new rail line from downtown Dallas to Ledbetter Street, a black community, was opened in 1996, and was extended to Plano, Texas, a predominantly white community, in the year 2001. That was very close to what Lateef Jakande, the UPN civilian governor, wanted for Lagos State in the second Republic, but the effort was thwarted by military government that usurped power on the New Year's Eve of 1983.

A new Highway 5 linking LBJ Freeway/Hwy 635 and Central Expressway/Hwy 75, just very similar to Ijora Highway in Lagos State, was under construction with an incentive package of $100,000 for each month ahead of schedule the contractor was able to beat the completion date.

American Airlines Center was constructed for the Dallas Mavericks basketball team, and the fifth terminal section of DFW Airport, one of the largest airports in the world, was almost finished. George Bush Highway 190/161 opened in 2002, and the following highways were extended: 635, the main road in Dallas, in 1999; Highway 30 East, 1999; Interstate Highway 20 in 1999 and many others.

Roads were constructed before development caught up with an area in Texas, with its cheap labor from Hispanic workers, who worked as if possessed, very determined at finishing any project. Despite all these shortcomings, it has never taken the love of Nigeria from me, and so it is with most Nigerians living abroad. Despite the frustrations, Nigerians love their country, just like Fela said in one of his song, "Suffering and smiling." In one internet opinion poll, Nigeria was reported as the country with the happiest people in the world. Nigeria loves to smile and always trusting in God, everything is always left at the mercy of God, even when they have criminals as government officials, they hope one day God will send a true government that will love the people and do right by them.

I have always loved my country of birth, and I have even loved my hometown Abeokuta more than anything. I pride myself as being fortunate to come from a City that was the first to have electricity in Africa in 1914. I always refer to my hometown as the first and best in everything, such as the first newspaper in Africa, by Rev. Henry Townsend "Iwe Iroyin", and the first church in Nigeria.

As a Yoruba man, I was even very proud of the attainment of the government of Papa Awolowo for establishing many firsts in Africa during his tenure as Premier of the Western Region. For example, like the first television, first Cocoa House, Liberty Stadium, and many others this became the bedrock of Nigeria's industrial revolution.

As a Nigerian, I was proud to be from a country with a bundle of talents, in areas of sports and academics. Easily, I could point to qualities of writers like Wole Soyinka and Chinua Achebe in any place. It was like the Yoruba adage that says *"Eniti O ba RI Oko Baba Elomi ani Oko Baba UN lo tobi ju,"* meaning "Your knowledge of life is just as wide and limited as the level of your exposure."

My return trip to Nigeria, and indeed Abeokuta, Ibadan, Sango Otta, and Lagos, changed and moved me to the point of tears. Right from the Lagos airport, I could see that the society looked hungry. The Lagos Airport employed staff to work in the restroom to hand over pieces of toilet paper for anyone trying to use the bathroom, with the hope of extracting tips by force, before one could use the restroom.

The baggage collection section was full of criminals, some luggage could not be found, and the customs and immigration officials preferred collecting dollars from passengers to extract money in dollars or foreign currency than to search the passengers. I thought to myself it was very easy to bring guns and drugs into the country; may God save Nigeria from terrorists.

The frontage of the airport was full of jobless people, ranging from fraudsters to those who had no business hanging around; it was a very frightening scene, which was not good for a first time visitor.

My son Peter was waiting at the airport for me. He looked taller, and looked exactly like me when I was his age, but slimmer.

"You need to eat burger." I gave him a hug and placed my Cowboy cap on his head.

I stole a look at him as the car he brought glided into the warm weather of Lagos, he had grown taller since I saw him, he had the smile of his grandmother, my height, and moves like a stallion just like my mother, and I felt a need to see my mother at Abeokuta immediately.

"How is Mama doing"? I asked.

"She is doing fine but she is out of her medication now" Peter said.

"I hope you brought some for her" He added.

"Yep, I have something special for you also" I said.

"Daddy, you know what I wanted most is to be with you in America" he said.

"You will and it will not be long" I said hopefully.

"Why is your sister not here? I asked.

"She had to take her final exams this morning" he said.

Abeokuta, the capital of Ogun State, did not look like a town prepared for development. Oke Ilewo road was clustered with the new generation of banks, cyber cafes, and some emergency car dealers. Some of them could not understand why would-be car buyers would ask the year of manufacture of a car, mileage, or history of the car; they were ignorant car dealers.

From Ibara to Sapon, I could see the city had a lot of potential, but the government seemed to be blind to it. To those in the government, turning cities to slums, with lots of people moving in an uncontrollable expansion, was development.

My visit to the Ministry of Commerce to meet with the Commissioner could not take place, the whole place looked deserted; the only fat and robust looking person in the ministry was the Commissioner of Commerce himself. They all looked tired, as if they were waiting for any opportunity to bleed the system. Joblessness was nothing new; wasted man-hours could be observed everywhere.

Ibadan, a trading town established by local warrior Lagelu during the old Oyo Empire, had remained what it was from the time I left Africa, with too many people struggling for the few amenities. Sango Otta, in Ogun State, was now clustered with people, like Oshodi in Lagos. Everything seemed rowdy, and dusty, and development was stagnant. I was amazed at how the former President Obasanjo could come to Sango Otta without observing or noticing what the people, his next-door community, were going through.

With all the clustered crowds and uncoordinated methods, including sporadic killings, with armed robbers having a field day without any challenge or concern from the government, the job of the internal security of each state was more than the federal police could handle alone. It was even more than State Police had prepared for. Time to try something different with local police system like we have in the United States of America, I thought to myself.

The country must take its cue from the American Police Administration, was my immediate thought. Each city should be allowed to have its own police force. The law to establish the city and state police must be written to prevent abuse by the politicians, and intervention from the Federal Government, unless there was a need for it.

The country, I believed, would start seeing the light at the end of the tunnel once city, state and federal police systems of Administration was adopted, much like the ones in the United States of

America. I believe there was nothing bad in copying what was good. A presidential system of democracy without decentralization of the police may not work in a country like Nigeria, I thought.

I got back to Murtala Mohammed Airport on January 1, 2004, only to be told my plane had left on December 31, 2003, which did not reflect well on World Airways. Thus began a 12-day ordeal at the Lagos Airport. We were lodged in a hotel that served only two types of food, Gari, or Eba, and rice throughout. Not all were so lucky, like a guy who was returning from Christmas vacation with his family of five and a friend from the USA. They gave out all their money and gifts to family and friends and what they had left was barely enough to get them to the airport before the flight was cancelled.

They were stranded at Lagos Airport with their two-month-old child. They could not get any help from their family or friends, who now realized the family, had nothing more to offer them. Most of the telephone calls made were not picked up; the only option for those who were American citizens was to turn to the U.S. Embassy for help.

The U.S. Embassy promised to help those who showed they were U.S. citizens only if they had good credit. Not many had. The attitude of the Embassy was simple; you came to your country, find help since most of us had dual citizenship. Some cried openly like babies, some turned their head in disbelief of the attitude of the Embassy officials and after many days of going to Eleke Crescent office of U.S. Embassy in Lagos without any help we left them alone to look for help on the street.

Twelve days went by; people were getting sick due to the unhygienic conditions. Sleeping like refugees on the airport benches and chairs, I was getting frustrated with the system. I was coughing and getting dehydrated.

"I know how you are feeling," said the Lagos Airport Chief Engineer.

"Oh no, you do not," I said.

"You are not the person sleeping on the benches; you are not the one with sick children or a job at stake, and at the end of the day you will go home. Oh no, you do not." I emphasized.

A group of us had assigned ourselves to meet with the Airport Authority; the Chief Engineer, who would be the airport staff member to handle this imbroglio. Everything was possible in Nigeria. The company executive that sold the dummy travel deal was never arrested nor prosecuted; he was infact receiving Presidential attention like a prince. The Nigeria press took interest in the plight of the people at the Airport; the government did not take a single action.

I was infected with bacteria due to unhygienic water and food, and was relieved to get, through my family in the USA, another one-way ticket back to Dallas through KLM Airlines. I thank God I did not lose my job like others who were victim of World Airways. Nigeria is not catching up with development like the rest of the world, and the world cannot wait for Nigeria. We must hurry up I thought to myself in frustration. While Nigeria as a people was asking the government for direction, the government seemed confused. Nigerians as usual, resulted to prayers to have a good government.

That was three years ago, and the Nigeria of 2007 was better than it was in 2003. Maybe God was listening after all. A new government had put in a lot of effort to clean the system, and the new President OBJ in his traditional wisdom of speaking had promised the country to see the fruits of Democracy. He worked so hard and hope was restored to his country but hope was not everything like the peasant of France before the revolution, Nigerians needed results. The establishment of Anti-Corruption Agency EFCC was indeed the tonic Nigeria needed to do right by the nation, Nigeria needed more to move the nation toward an egalitarian society.

It was a very bright morning, on November 19, 2007. I woke up with a lot of strength in me. I was looking forward to the end of the semester of a program I had started at Corsicana, Texas after a bitter and shocking experience with another program in Waco, Texas, which had derailed my original plans for a year.

With the clinical exposure I received, and spending time with the elderly in a rehabilitation center as part of the program, I learned to occupationally treat patients with CVA (stroke) and TBI (Traumatic Brain Injury) and other degenerative diseases. I could see the need to care for the elderly. I was learning more each day and I could see the effort and progress these patients were making daily to regain their functional mobility and the activities of daily living.

Each day I thought of similar projects that might benefit the aged in Africa. My mind was on my parents and the bitter, but fortunate experience in

1992 when my father had his stroke. His treatment and recovery was the collective responsibility of the family and the neighborhood. Our limited knowledge of daily activity of daily living and instrument of daily living had stretched his life for another 15 years. It was like the story in the Bible when a sick man asked God to extend his life; the Bible said his prayers were answered.

Sometimes I could see the Bible more like the living testimony of events of everyday life. One could relate each functional event of life to the stories in the first published book on earth, first compiled 167 years after the death of Jesus Christ. The Bible became the best book I ever read. Perhaps it was due to the manner my teachers in the high school had taught us. At one time, some of us were so knowledgeable in the words of God that we thought of becoming Pastors. One of us did, and he became one of the best known faces in Nigeria today, Pastor Tunde Bakare of the Latter Rain Church.

A week before the death of my father I had talked to a childhood friend from Nigeria, Segun Oni. His mother had died and he requested me to come home and be with him during the burial as was the custom.

"Mama will be buried by December 12th "Segun Oni said.

"I had planned to be in Nigeria December 19th for the Christmas" I said.

"Change your date to December 8th or so" Segun further requested.

"I will be there for you my friend on that day" I said.

His mother was very close to us, she used to sell roasted plantain when we were very young and Segun became a good friend because we could eat plantain for free; Mama never knew all these but we have been friends from elementary school. He had progressed to the position of local or county chief engineer and his beautiful black wife Bunmi, a staff nurse and very respectful and loving lady; together they remained one of the best promising couples of our group.

As his mother advanced in age, she moved to Abeokuta and was living with her son as is the custom of Yoruba and Africa at large. There was nothing like nursing home for us. I changed my travel date to December 8th in anticipation of standing by my friend, but as fate would have it I never knew I would be doing the same for my father.

Earlier in the morning of November 19th 2007, I had talked to my cousin Pappy Jay, who lived in Durham, North Carolina. We asked about each other's family, work, and also talked about the events at home, like every other Nigerian living abroad. I left my phone in the car while I was at work that day.

I came out during lunchtime to check my messages, and I had ten missed calls, all from Nigeria. My heart was pounding; I could feel my heart beating against my ribs.

I was still trying to check the messages when the phone rang again. My heart skipped. The same number of the missed ten calls was on the phone again.

"We took Papa to the hospital this morning, and I will be calling back to let you know the outcome," and the phone went dead.

But I knew the voice; it was my brother at home Augustine. He knew I would recognize his voice, he felt there was no need for introduction. My mind went to money. I was not working full time because of the school program. How much would it cost, and who would be his doctor this time around? I called my two brothers in Texas to tell them of the new development and to contact home urgently.

Three hours later, the phone rang again, and this time I was no longer thinking about the hospital charges. The mirror was broken; the glass has been shattered into pieces.

"The old man is gone," the caller said.

Such was the way we broke news of death among my tribe.

"How and when did he finally die?" I asked.

"Papa had a slight headache for two days, and had asked two of the neighbors to take him to the hospital. After undergoing preliminary tests in the hospital, he requested for his Priest to pray and give him the last Holy Communion as a Catholic. He talked quietly with Mama and me," the caller said. He knew it was time for him to go. He prayed for all, and a few minutes later he went into cardiac arrest. He died around 3:00 p.m. November 19, 2007," Deola explained quietly, and waited for me to absorb the shock.

I was quiet for a couple of minutes and thoughts over everything about my father, his struggles, his sacrifices and how he denied himself basic needs to take care of us his children, the tears came down on my cheeks as I sobbed alone in my car. I had no one to comfort me except the dangling catholic rosary in front of my inner mirror. I held onto it and cried and cried.

"I have to travel to Nigeria to bury my father as it is the custom of my tribe" I said to Mrs. Anita Lane the program Director at Navarro College Corsicana, Texas.

'You could be excused for the remaining three days of the session" she said.

"Accept my sympathy and that of the Department" she said with pity in a soft but shaky voice. I could not look her in the eyes to avoid tears as I walked out of her office.

I was at my regular work at Kindred hospital in Dallas, Texas the same night to tidy up my request to go "Home." All the night shift staff was sympathetic, they contributed money and those without money showed kindness and sympathy.

We held a wake keeping at my brother's apartment in Dallas, all his friends came. He had a bunch of them, all of them looking trim and cute. They all prayed for the repose of the death and for God to grant him eternal rest in His Kingdom.

December 8th as earlier arranged, became the day I went to Nigeria for the funeral. The Old Man was buried December 14, 2007 as a Roman Catholic Christian with all the paraphernalia of Catholic rites. He left behind my mother and six children: I, my two sisters, and three brothers and grandchildren.

It was the first Christmas in our household without the old man. We did not even know how to go about it or the directions to follow. My oldest sister was still trying to accept the new responsibility, but Yoruba traditions put a man in charge.

My mother was still not healthy. She could not even walk. She was torn between the shock of Papa's death and her health, and I was still dazed with the development and reality. I could not hold the tears anymore. I was crying like a baby, even though they say men don't cry. I am not sure if the propagator of the analogy realizes the importance of losing a father. I cried and cried, and asked questions that I could not get answers to.

The extended family and neighbors stood by us like a rock. My uncles and cousin Ade Shoyoye were all there on a daily basis, but it was not enough to replace the absence of our father. As days went by, the number of callers reduced. I took my mother to my house to live with me. Her health was my concern, she took her medications on time and I started seeing positive results due to her improvement.

It was time for me to get back to America. A family meeting to discuss the welfare of our mother and those living with her was arranged and concluded. I hired a nurse aide for my mother, who was generously paid, because I felt no amount was too much to spend when it came to one's mother. The second week into the New Year, I left Africa, but the tears and emptiness never stopped. Papa's death and his absence recreated me. It made me to grow even more in knowledge and traditional wisdom, but never could it fill the vacuum that was created by his absence on the day he closed his eyes. The tears never stopped. Each day I remember the whole events, I still shed tears, even as I am writing this.

Papa died as a committed Catholic, and stood with the God his mother showed him from the day he was taken from the village to Ibadan by his uncle, after the death of his twelve brothers and sisters.

Everything works for the glory of God, they say. I was already thinking on a daily basis of how I could spend Christmas with my parents. It was almost three years when last I saw him. Each day had been marred with arguments over some of the family's needs and responsibilities.

Ten years in America had affected my often-assumed tough measures on my brothers and sisters. I had learned to be level headed, cool and calm, and listen more than just forming an opinion about events or actions. I guess I was growing in age and wisdom, and my new environment had affected my African culture and tradition.

I was struggling between being what I am and what I was. The middle ground between the two was often misunderstood for gentility, which it was not. I was more patient with life and at peace with God.

PART EIGHT

I Can Feel Your Pain

Part Eight
I Can Feel Your Pain

*He looked directly at the camera, as if talking
to a particular individual, but in fact he was
indirectly communicating to millions of viewers.
He said in a shaky voice,
"I can feel your pain."*

-President Bill Clinton

I Can Feel Your Pain

❖ ❖ ❖

Honestly, the health care industry was the last field I thought I would find very interesting, not to even make a career out of. I never liked the hospital environment, having grown up in Africa. Ibadan was the largest and most populous city in Africa in the sixties. JP Clack, a renowned poet, described the city in his poem, *Ibadan,* as "flung and scattered among the seven hills like a broken china plate in the sun." It was also described by one of the archivists at the National Archive inside the University of Ibadan, where I had worked in the seventies, as a city with "uncontrollable expansion." As it was road and streets were not planned or tarred.

In the fifties and sixties, African hospitals were not associated with cleanliness like we see today. The mere smell of the hospital environment was enough to discourage a person from getting or seeking care.

The terrible hospital odor had very quickly made me well as soon I arrived at the hospital gate. Besides, I never liked being injected or vaccinated at all. To show my disgust and hatred for the hospital environment and the bitter experiences in my early years as a student of Lisabi Grammar school, I had written an article about the terrible medical environment in a tribute to the King of my home town when he died a few years ago. It was widely circulated in the newspapers, and read as follows:

". . . The only hospital then, at Ijaiye, in the heart of Abeokuta, was associated with incompetent performances. The doctors then were not willing to make an effort to save lives. A small bone fracture caused in a motor accident would result in instant amputation. Many lost their legs, including one very popular athlete in one of the secondary schools in Abeokuta in 1971; John, a track athlete, was the hope of the city for the coming all-secondary-schools competition in the Western Region.

On our way back from Comprehensive High School Aiyetoro to participate in the inter-house sports competition, we had a motor accident. John was one of the victims rushed to Ijaiye Hospital Abeokuta for medical attention. His left leg was amputated without a second opinion or parent approval. The whole of Abeokuta City indigenes wept. Such were the untold horrors and hardship brought too many homes in the seventies." Functional rehabilitation as physical, occupational or speech therapy was alien to us then.

It wasn't until I arrived in the United States of America, in 1996, that my opinion of the hospital work environment and health care industry and sanitation began to change positively. I always had the phobia that someone might try something funny on me if I visited a hospital. I was one of those who was never sick or visited a hospital.

As soon as I returned from Africa in 2004, my position as Manager with 7-Eleven was threatened. The flight had been cancelled, due to a disagreement with the Lagos end of the deal from World Airways of Georgia State in USA.

I was coughing and sneezing, and suffered a sore throat, which was associated with food poisoning and increasing weakness to my immune system. But my friends believed it was religiously associated with witchcraft, of eating from an unfriendly environment. You see, in Africa, nothing ever happens without a reason. Someone must be blamed for everything. We started looking and searching for those who may not have been happy about my homecoming. It was funny, but I knew better. However, it was useless convincing people of my new belief that nothing, but simply a change of environment and a weakened immune system, could be responsible. I did not receive any shots or vaccinations before rushing home, years out of Africa had affected my immunity, but I had felt I had to play along with their beliefs.

Three weeks after I returned, I was still unable to go to work. I lost my position to another retail manager, and was upset with a system that would not guarantee my job in case of sickness or a situation beyond my control. I started thinking of a profession where there would always be a need in my adopted country; the health care industry was becoming more acceptable to many of us foreigners.

Foreigners' accents would not be a barrier to finding jobs if one could specialize in any healthcare field, which was what most Africans settled for after many years of looking for management or white collar positions that would never be given out, because of color or accent. Each time most Africans applied for a job and a phone interview was scheduled, once an accent was noted, that would be the end of conversation.

"We will get back to you," was a polite way of saying we don't need you . . .

It took many of us years to come to this reality of looking beyond our academic qualifications from Africa to pursue another career in America. The hope of using my MBA Degree from the University of Ibadan was diminishing with the reality of not getting the job befitting of my academic attainment. All I could see were medical and Health care personnel from Africa and other nationals doing fine and those with pure academic background scrambling for the crumbs in the land assumed to flow with milk and honey or land of opportunities.

Nursing as a career was number one, after respiratory inhalation, to most foreigners, but physical therapy and occupational therapy were among the lists on my consideration. Eventually, I decided on occupational therapy, simply because the program was designed for people with family responsibilities, who needed to be able to work as well as attend classes.

In the meantime, I was working in the hospital in various capacities as a wound care technician, as well as patient care technician, and sometimes as a phlebotomist. It was an experience that helped me to realize how superior the medical system is in the United States, compared to most developing countries.

Patients remain the focus of the hospitals. In fact, on face value doctors hired hospitals to take care of their patients, being "on call" and remaining the leaders of the health profession. Nurses, who carry the bulk of the work in the hospital, work hard, and in most cases work double-shifts. One little mistake was all it requires to lose one's license to practice in the healthcare field, particularly in the state of Texas. You could lose your job like a flip of coin if you received too many complaints from the patients.

The Patient's Bill of Rights, Health Insurance and Private and Protective Act (HIPPA), and other medical regulations help to ensure good medical attention for patients. To the system, it is a business relationship, nothing more; "consumer is the king," as they say in marketing. However, in the health care industry, patients have the right to refuse treatment; you cannot force it upon them. In the medical field as practitioners, two things reign supreme: the patients and the doctors, all others must toe the line.

Some patients may irritate you to the point of making you angry, but you must remain focused. "Be professional," they say, even to the point of being hit by the patients. My first week as a wound care technician was touchy, but I was able to understand the system, which tends to take the side of the patient, rather than the staff.

My patients often told me stories of how they ended up in the hospital, and some of the stories could be very funny or sometimes unimaginable. Some were injured through carelessness, while some were self-inflicted and others by events beyond their control. I realize it could be me on the sick bed there; I was always very compassionate to their stories.

A lady became paralyzed when she was just getting out of the bathtub. She fell backward and had her spinal cord damaged, another patient asked his father for a Harley Davidson as a birthday present when he turned 21. The second day, he had an accident and was paralyzed from the neck down; C4 cervical vertebrae, he was only 34 years old when he became my patient.

Another very touchy story was that of a patient who had his entire lower extremity removed. He had no legs, no butt, just the head, neck, and stomach. I was his wound care technician, and was not properly briefed on what to expect. I thought his legs were hidden inside the mattress. I was asking him to turn over, and then I saw his condition. I was shaken, both in body and faith, but he was very understanding and helped me out. His wound was at the tail end of his spinal cord. He had been mistakenly shot from behind by a gang of criminals on his way from work. He was a father of five, and his children all came to see him on a daily basis. His room was decorated with flowers and affection. By the time he died, he had been in and out of the hospital for the last 25 years.

Some patients tended to be mean to their caregivers for various reasons, from race to religion or sex. Some just hated the caregiver because of the color of his or her skin, or for being a black man in a profession they believed should be exclusively for whites or women. Men had to struggle to keep up with the politics of the job. It was a different ball game entirely each day on the job; I had to display extreme carefulness and respect for my patients.

Another lady, who had been my patient from the day she was admitted into the hospital, had become very fond of me, and despite her limited communication skills, we still talked. I made her laugh and became the only person she would trust, with everything from grooming to upper body activities and to dressing her wounds. She was a quadriplegic patient and on a DNR, which means "do not resuscitate" in case the patient goes into a coma, or coding, like we say in the medical field. But inside her, she harbored hatred for people of color; she could not trust us, and would do anything to destroy any caregiver that became victim to her cold mood, but I could not understand.

One caregiver was not aware of how she felt because of the nature of her condition. He tried to preach the Bible to her, and in her anger she accused him of molesting her. I was the only guy that could help to straighten out a situation which could have caused the caregiver to lose his license or even go to jail.

I visited with her and told her of the need to ensure openness in her attitude. I told her how God still loved her, despite her condition, and that whatever happened might be a preparation for a better place with the Lord. I reminded her of the Book of Romans, Chapter 12, when the Apostle Paul said, and "if possible be at peace with all." She requested me to read the whole chapter to her. I did.

She cried as I placed the Bible down, and I understood her pain and years of misery. She was in love with a man, who had taken her on a trip to Las Vegas, Nevada. They had stopped to see the beauty of the Hoover Dam and on the way, they had a car accident in which he died instantly and she was left paralyzed. She was then 21 years old with youth on her side; that had been her case for the past 31 years; she died three days after our talk. I believe she was at peace with the Lord before the transition, because she made peace with the caregiver. So I thought.

Each day in the hospital, I became closer to God in my faith. I tried to offer something new to my patients. In many cases, some would throw objects at their caregiver, not understanding that they needed to be diverted from medication. Some tried to be more understanding and loving, but it was tough on them.

If you looked well, you could see the lines of pain on their faces. Most of them, when asked to describe their pain on a scale of one to ten, will say seven out of ten. Some will ask for morphine or hydrocodone, probably the toughest pain medications in the world, every two hours instead of four hours, the minimum. The effect of these medications could damage their kidney leading to dialysis, sometimes worst than what brought them to the hospital.

Some of the patients, despite their conditions, still wanted things done in their own way. In most cases, their own way would be time-wasting, and would not conform to the appropriate standards. Some of them had had their hormones altered due to medication; women grew beards and mustaches like men, a situation that was strange to me initially. In some situations, I had to shave female patients.

A female in her fifties, at first appearance, looked like a man. Back home in Africa, she would have been labeled a "witch," particularly because of the way she looked wild, with a surrounding mustache, and a deep voice. "I will be glad if you can do this for me," she said, in a deep voice that made the two of us in the room sound like men. She had requested the funny looking beard be shaved. It was difficult, initially, to shave her face. I did, but my first impression of her remained with me for a long time.

When I eventually picked occupational therapy as a career, I knew it was my calling. I loved my patients, and loved doing the work. It helped to express my inner self as a Christian, and my conflict in searching for a relationship with God became whole, and I met a peace of mind. My dream to have my own business never died, as years later, along with an old friend, we established Staffing Agency for the healthcare industry and a tax office in Irving, Texas.

The search was over, and my Christian faith grew like the Biblical faith of Israelis, though it took me years to find peace with the Lord. But the journey was worth the route.

PART NINE

Religion as a Question

Part Nine
Religion as a Question

Religion as a Question

❖ ❖ ❖

Unlike Christianity, which holds its origin and foundation in Judaism, the Yoruba method of serving God credits its existence to the roles given to the gods, like Orisha Obatala and Ifa in the creation of both mankind as well as regular human beings. Yoruba religion seems to be much more moralistic than Christianity, which is based on the grace of Jesus Christ. However, like Judaism, Yoruba religion also has its idea of how the Supreme God, which we called Olodumare, created heaven and earth.

The Yoruba nation, probably the most populous single African tribe in the world, based in the south of Sahara, was described by the Dallas Texas Museum of Art as having the greatest spiritual and social impact on over 76 million blacks in America, Latin America, and within Europe, including Africa itself. We are a people with a proud and envious culture, which often find it difficult to separate our ways of life from our religion based on intermediaries to the supreme God, Olodumare, or in a simpler form,

Olorun, the owner of the great sky. This is often reflected in the names given to children, indicating how and why they are blessed, just like my name, Idowu, the first son after a set of twins. It is also evident in certain circumstances of death and birth, love and relationships, all which are attributed to gods, concluding that nothing can happen without the approval of the gods.

In the Yoruba religion and belief system, all angels obey God's command, none is evil, there is no Satan, and all are in charge of certain duties assigned by Olodumare, to whom all shall return. This is the belief of my people, the descendants of Oduduwa, the progenitor of the people of lower Niger. We did not believe Satan or Esu had the capacity to challenge or mess up the work of God Olodumare. Satan and other angels work with the approval of Almighty God

Christianity teaches about the existence of the Trinity: God the Father, God the Son, and God the Holy Spirit, and Jesus, the Son of God, who like Daniel will come to judge. The Christian faith further teaches about humility and service to mankind in exchange for the Kingdom of God, in which faith in Jesus is the only route to the Promised Land. The religion uses the foundation of Judaism to broaden the minds of the followers, as Jesus claimed he had not come to change the law, but to enforce it, and these laws were routed in Jewish foundation and religion. What was confusing to all was that "He" actually came to introduce a new way of serving God, which was alien to the beliefs of the people of his generation, like the Sanhedrin and other opinionated leaders of his time. Among the Yoruba, the idea of getting to

God is not a one-man route, as it is in the Christian faith. They believe that good work to mankind will determine your qualification to heaven.

Ulli Beier (1997) like many West African people, the Yoruba practice several religions, so no single one can be declared their universal belief. Many Yoruba people in today's society have converted to Christianity or Islam. Even though this is the case, one look at a Yoruba ritual will convince you that there is another, more fundamental ideology at the core of Yoruba beliefs. The ideology that is present here is called *Orisa*. Orisa is the traditional Yoruba religion that has been practiced for generations. The Christian faith, apart from the trinity, is no different than Judaism. Each one of these religions has its roots in one or two things.

Christianity has its roots with Judaism, and Yoruba religion has its in Oduduwa, and his relationship with Orisha, Obatala, and the god of creation who was always dressed in a white garment, and Ifa, the god of divinity, capable of foretelling the future. There are also Shango, the god of thunder, also in charge of justice, and Esu, the angel in charge of discipline, in case one refuses to obey the command of Olodumare or any of the traditional local gods, like Obatala, whose followers must not drink palm wine or dress in any color but white, or Ifa Oracle after warning.

In all, the Yoruba religion is very fascinating, but the beauty has been eroded with the advent of Christianity and Islam. However, it remains unshaken in the minds, souls, and fundamentals of the people of the lower Niger community.

Bolaji Idowu (1969) indicated in his book, _God in Yoruba Belief,_ that the responsibilities of both religions are diverse and creative in uplifting societal development towards having compassion and empathy for one another, and that in both, judgment should be the last of events among fellow human beings.

McBride Richards (1997), the author of "_Lives of the Popes_", described and compared the life of the Pope, the head of the Pontiff, to that of a monarch. The day one disagrees with the Pope, who, it is believed, can do no wrong; one is excommunicated from the Catholic Church. This practice is exactly what led to the separation and breakdown of the Christian faith into many denominations; hence, they say "You can be more Catholic than the Pope."

The Church of England came as a result of marital relationships, those of the King of England and divorce situations. The same can be said of all the new generational churches, including the Pentecostals and of recent Scientologists.

Unlike the Yoruba religions, which separate responsibilities and control among the gods, the Christian faith tends to unite everything under the umbrella of Christ Jesus. Sometimes, I am tempted to believe that there is no democracy in Christianity. You either believe or you are a non-believer, and once a non-believer, you are no longer a follower of Christ, as simple as ABC. What, then, is the future of both religions?

As Western education continues to make a mockery of traditional religion and modes of worship, the Christian faith tends to gain the upper hand,

and the level of belief of the people of lower Niger continues to shift to the western ways of life. One cannot but summarizes the two, Christianity and Yoruba religions, in the language of Professor Bolaji Idowu. As mentioned above, "the responsibilities of both religions are both diverse and creative to uplifting the societal development towards having feeling and empathy for one another, and judgment should be the last event among fellow human beings."

Unlike this author, writers from other religions tend to see non-Christians as idol and fetish worshippers. The true answer to who can serve God better in the mind of all is that no one is right. No one is wrong. It is a win-win situation, and no one should feel any animosity towards other religions.

The above is an indication that religion is in the mind and control of the generation that believes there is a force beyond the control of mankind, and their thinking that the force radiates the existence of the universe. The same force may be the Supreme Being, in which the Yoruba called Olorun or Olodumare, and Edos called Osanobuwa, the people of Benin Republic called Nanabuluku, and in which Jesus Christ, the Son of God, is believed to be the only route to Heaven according to the Christian faith.

In all my life, I had taken the love of God for granted. I never bothered to explore beyond the little Christian Roman Catholic background I had as a struggling child of the environment within my life. For those of us in the high school, living in the school hostel was a different game entirely; we were forced to wear white long pants, long sleeve shirts, white tennis shoes and clean socks to attend the Anglican Church despite our backgrounds. I was a Catholic, and the Anglican system was often strange to me.

We marched through the street of Ijaiye in Abeokuta to Erunbe, the soft, sport church of Revered Lapese Ladipo, the school principal, along with my buddy Lobito Brown, called Femi Sobowale, Ebenezer Sopade, and Emmanuel Adekunte, also called Sample. It was very humorous, but interesting, to get out of the school hostel in the jungle areas of the Lisabi Grammar School.

We were made to listen to the Anglican preacher's monotonous voice delivering his boring message. During school vacation, either there was also another boring Catholic one-hour program at St. Gabriel Catholic Church at Mokola, or the Cathedral at Oke Padre Ibadan. Boring and nothing of a challenge, the program usually ended when Holy Communion was served. I never really felt like a Christian or understood what the concept was all about. I considered attending church more of a ritual and obligation, not knowing the reasons for it.

I was never a perfect or serious Christian in my youth. I remember a scene in the Sixties when my brothers and I were to go to church, which conflicted with a good Indian movie to be shown at Scala Cinema that morning. My option was clear, and it was the movie. My father decided to have me disciplined in his own way. The very first slap landed heavily on my face, and it was like seeing stars, so I decided to play on his emotions. I pretended as if I had lost my sight. He was shaken, as our neighbors and my father thought I had gone blind.

The news of my assumed blindness had gone around the whole community like a wild wind, and each person kept adding to the story, one version even claimed that I was paralyzed. Some said my eyeballs came out. People were coming to see the man who could have done such a horrible thing to his first son. It was different versions to most people. I pretended for more than two hours. My Dad was shaken, and he never touched me again. I could see his love for me from his fear, and despite his toughness, he was a kind father in his heart. This parenting style was common among African fathers, to "be tough; don't openly show your love attitude."

"Can you see my hand?" He asked in a shaky voice.

"No sir." I said with a calculated, trembling voice. I had seen enough of Indian movies to know how to act.

"How about my face?" my father asked again, while he was moving his hand left-to-right across my face.

"Where is your face, Papa?" I reached for his chest, pretending his face was within my reach.

At that juncture, my mother could not take it anymore. She stepped in and asked in a very soft and loving voice,

"Idowu, my husband, can you see me, your mother?"

She addressed me in the way the Yoruba talked to their favorite son. She kept chanting sorrowfully the praise of Idowu, in the traditional way my grandmother used to do with her god of twins.

It was more like a conditional fight between the gods of twins and my father now. I had compassion for my mother and did what most kids would have done. I started crying, but still added some effects to my tricks.

"Mama," I said. "Do you think I am blind because everything is black?" I said in tears, and decided to push it further with my next question, which shocked my parents.

"Can a blind person still go to school?" I was asking more than she could answer. She joined me in crying also.

After two hours of demonstration of these multi-step pranks, I decided to ease their worries. I told my mother I could see a little bit. That was the last time Papa disciplined me. He drew me closer to himself in some cases. We went to the movies together; maybe he was trying to appease the gods of twins, but I got my freedom. I later realized he had a serious conversation with my grandmother.

I had grown up in a community where faith could be tested, and some had not been sincere. At Mountain of Mercy Church, the pastor ordered all the women to deposit their jewelry in the church because God had told him to destroy it. He took all the jewelry, sold it, bought a new Land Rover jeep, and said the vehicle had come from heaven. Everyone came from far and wide to see the vehicle that had descended, like Elijah's chariot, from heaven.

Surprisingly, nobody was bold or knowledgeable enough to ask to see the vehicles VIN number to determine the year of purchase or who could have bought the vehicle. We all, in our ignorance, believed the "chariot of Elijah", until years later when he impregnated a lady in church. The unsuspecting female members saw the light, to say the least. The church, because of this incident, broke into two factions.

When I was a business student, I started searching for the missing gap in my spiritual world. I attended many churches of various denominations. Some seemed funny, like the Celestial Church, where it was forbidden to have your shoes on. Interestingly enough, and unknown to members, the founder could not find shoes in a size to fit into his very long feet, hence, he decreed the removal of shoes in his church. But that was not my reason for joining this church. The church members could dance, and their flowing white gowns, called "sutana", were beautiful on the ladies and young men.

To approach ladies in the Celestial Church for relationships was very simple in those days. All you needed to say was "Hallelujah o", slang my friend Segun Coker, who now lives in Canada, still finds interesting today. It was all fun in those days.

I was very emotional about music, and the feeling behind the accordion, the ringing tone of percussion, flow of beautiful voices and melodies of the church took me into the fold.

I was amazed and flabbergasted by the revelations and visions of the prophets. They purported to see the future and told us about imaginary enemies, but all in all, they made members depend on them for decisions making. In so doing, the data base of the congregation increased and members were all subjected to fear of the future. They began to lack independence and their ability to move and make decisions became questionable. I became friends with most of the young prophets of my age. They found me very easy to get along with and knowledgeable about life, because I had studied Religion for my GCE Advanced level.

Unknown to them, I was searching. I was not ready to have anything less than perfection. They were using their spiritual gifts to get women, and told me if I needed any, they would provide a vision that would help out. Members were made to drink "green water" and some funny looking olive oil, with different types of candles sometimes planted in some unusual places, in the nights and mostly by the riverside in fighting imaginary enemies and sorting favors, I was disappointed in the Celestial Church; my spiritual growth and fulfillment remained unmet, so I moved on.

I could remember, in my curiosity for spiritual search, a church in Lagos, with red garment in which all members said nothing except "Jah". People in Lagos sometimes jokingly said if you slapped them or motor vehicle accident with them, all they would say was "Jah", and move on. I was too scared to enter the Church, but never stopped wondering what they were doing inside their Sanatorium.

In between all these spiritual movements, I was still attending the Catholic Church, even though I was spiritually unfulfilled. It was the foundation church of my family, and I was told my grandmother was the first Roman Catholic in our family. Sometimes

I attended the Redeemed Christian Church of God, a Pentecostal gathering because of deep prayers and commitment to the scriptures. They could pray and make you feel like Christ will come down immediately. In faith, He does. But all the churches are favorites of the areas that ask for your money, nothing more. Hence, Pastors with poor congregation lives in affluence with members in abject poverty that was strange to me.

The search for a living church to connect with, took me too many in Dallas, Texas, including an all-white church. A white lady thought, in her ignorance, that Africans were not Christians, and she wanted to introduce a black man from Africa to Christ. I went to the church, and to my surprise I was the only black face in the sanctuary, and they were so prejudiced that no one sat close to me. From the way the Pastor was preaching, I realized I knew more about the Bible than the Pastor himself; he was not preaching about Jesus, he was talking about race. By the time it was time for members to hug each other as was the custom in most churches, I had no one to turn to I was by myself.

A friend I met in a Dallas library invited me to all-black Pilgrim Rest Baptist Church on Haskell Street in downtown Dallas, Texas.

"You need to hang out with black folks," he said.

I did.

Surprisingly, I saw a photograph of Black Jesus strangely displayed in the Church, and never stopped wondering if Jesus from Nazareth and Israel could have been a black man. I was not after color, but spiritual connection with God. The church to me was more about the color than the preaching of Jesus Christ, with that conclusion I moved on. I was looking for a church where all races would be represented.

I continued my search for another place of worship that would fit my spiritual connection, and it ended with a visit to DFW New Beginning Church in Irving, Texas. It was a church for all races, more like the United Nations. The pastor, Larry, was my ideal preacher. He could bring Jesus to your side like having a one-on-one discussion. The color of your skin was not the point, but the love of God and sweet fellowship of the powerful Holy Spirit, directed by Jesus Christ.

He was a drug addict who became a Christian and was led by a Hispanic Christian to see the light of Christ. His life story was very unique and I could see my own journey in the way he walked to God himself; I knew this would be my home church as I walked to the altar to give my life to Christ. After I had attended the church for three weeks, I knew it was time to be inclusive in the activity of the church.

As I stood up and walked down the aisle, tears came down my cheeks, my soul was relieved, and I knew what it is to be born again. I remembered my first born again roommate in 1975 and wondered if he had seniority over me in the Kingdom of God. I was at peace with myself and God. I do not care and was never afraid of any negative forces or the future again.

I realized the love of Jesus Christ for me more than anything in the world. I was even taller in real life than the tiny gods of twins in dark corners of my grandmother's bedroom that had affected my faith and dreams many years of my life and was wondering how on earth anyone could be serving a god that was not even higher than one's knees. I knelt down at the altar; I thanked God the Father, the Son, and the Holy Spirit for giving me another chance to see His love for me again, and walking with me, not against me, through the journey of my Christian rebirth. I dropped my middle Idowu name and never to be associated with any gods or contact with fetish beliefs.

The same feeling of strong rebirth was also rekindled in me when I visited the Times Square Church in New York years later; between the two churches and my long background in the search for spiritual connection with Christ, I discovered the difference between fake and original, between the truth and reality, and I knew why Jesus Christ was comfortable with sinners like me and many others in my position. I realized wealth or riches should never be measured by physical properties or stocks, but by winning souls for Jesus and trusting in the Lord for providing the "daily bread" not tomorrow because it will take care of itself.

About the Author

Z **ents Sowunmi** is employed with the Department of Defense, Warrior Transition Battalion, Fort Bliss. He is also the President of Korloki, Inc. a staffing, technical training, and consulting corporation based in Irving, Texas. A prolific writer, having written numerous articles and papers on a variety of topics, this is one of his best writings where he shares parts of his life journey. Zents' insights helped many individuals discover truths that have made a difference in their careers, marriages, and relationships, including misconceptions about Africa. Changing a person's frown to a smile is what he is known for. His kind words, charm, and wit have helped to brighten someone's day, especially the individuals he serve, and dear friends he cherishes. He is also the author of **What Happened to Our Democracy**. He lives in Texas. His books are available worldwide.

11713129R00124

Made in the USA
Charleston, SC
15 March 2012